New Directions

Book One

By: Alexander Hudson Akins

Middle-ground Publishing

Chapter One

<u>A Newfound Friend</u>

Can you tell me a story?" I asked, looking up at Grapefruit. She smiled, "Sure!" An exciting emotion filled the room as she began, "A long, long time ago, this world was split in two, dragons and gryphons lived separate from each other, to avoid war, until one day, the princess of the dragons, Vence, and the prince of the gryphons, Celtic, fell in love.

They had eight heirs, who were the first of each of the tribes, living today; they were all hybrids of gryphon and dragon. Their existence was strictly forbidden, so that ended up starting a war.

Years after that, our species came to be. There are very few purebred dragons and gryphons in our world today, so we carried on the gryphon name." I smiled and pleaded for the rest of the story. She melted and agreed,

"Our species had the head and body of a dragon, but feather wings with a gryphon's lion tail. We got our talons and body shape from our dragon ancestors, and our feathers, and sharp eyesight, from our gryphon ancestors.

Each tribe has a special gift, some have the ability to create a void, that can contain any living species near it. But some, who make the void will pass out and become weak, for an extended amount of time. Some have special camouflage they can't control - their minds connect with our surroundings and to others, it will look like they aren't there... others have the ability to make sharper turns and breathe hotter fire.

She continued, "Desert Gryphons have the ability to create massive sandstorms! Sea Gryphons can breathe underwater and talk to fish, while Mountain Gryphons were given the power to speak to other animals. Finally, our tribe was given the special power of magic, to curse or bless, any other, or themselves. Our blood is known to curse the one who spills it.

Finally, all of us can breathe fire... but, that's all my little gryphonnet, now get some sleep." I smiled and closed my eyes, welcoming the dearly wanted slumber.

The light shone bright into my eyes. "Ugh... what happened?" I groaned in annoyance, blinking my eyes open. As my vision cleared, I walked outside. I looked up to see a huge towering boulder with another gryphon-hybrid laying, trapped underneath.

They'll probably yell at me for not being strong enough to pick up the boulder... I should just leave. Ugh, but the poor gryphon - okay just this once, I told myself, shoving my horns under the boulder in an attempt to raise it up off the poor being.

Their eyes opened, as I pushed the boulder over the hill, "Who are you, to be helping me... the great Noirscales!?" they growled, in immediate defense.

"I-uh-uhm-I, uh,-I gotta go" I stuttered, and rushed off. I need to find somewhere to be alone. My mind murmured, as I rushed off.

I continued on my way, and found a small cave, which seemed to be an abandoned home. Inside, I saw scrolls… covered in cobwebs. Oh! Books! There was a book placed on the shelf, titled, A Dark Roar, on the front cover, was a dark blue, Night-ice gryphon. It reminded me of my favorite book. I should probably head back to tell that gryphon where they are, I thought.

I had a quiet feeling of guilt in my chest, so, I spread my wings and flew back to the area, the sun baked my feathers. Soon after, I noticed that gryphon, talking to another. I ducked down, and landed, swiftly, on my talons. Suddenly, it seemed, I had forgotten how to talk, "uh-uhm... Hi" I stammered, as they turned to look at me.

"You're the one that lifted that boulder, then flew away!" one of them said, smiling, and pointing their talons at me. "Um, yeah... uh, by the way, you're right in between the Sky Palace and the village down by the lake" I said. They seemed pleased to hear that. "I'm Ryuu, by the way." they commented.

I nodded and smiled. "I'm Ruby," the gryphon next to Ryuu announced, gleefully. Ryuu beamed. He was happy that he was near his home. After chatting with these two gryphons, for a while, I realized how hungry I was. It had been so long since I last ate. So, I invited them to come with me and we soon arrived at my village, in the Jungle Kingdom.

I instantly felt better. The succulent scent of the growing fruits, the lush green color of the leaves, and the complex structure of the village, was comforting. The village was quite beautiful. Ruby and Ryuu followed me, past shop vendors with warm spices, fruit, trees. and flowers. Charming cobblestone, on the street, clatters as village gryphons ran across it. "I'm friends with a sweet gryphon, who lives over there." I said, as I took flight again, and Ruby and Ryuu followed.

We soared down through the trees; Ruby and I, ran into each other... twice, as our wings seemed too big and broad to fit between some of them.

But Ryuu could read the place like a scroll and just passed through, easily. Soon enough, we reached the hut, belonging to my friend. I knocked on the door, expecting to be waiting for a response, but not a moment later, my friend answered the door. "Greetings to you, Grapefruit. These are my new friends, Ruby and Ryuu." I stated, giving her a big smile, as we made our way inside.

Grapefruit's hut was trimmed with vines across the top of the walls, meeting the familiar, dark, wood roof, common in this area. She had long, blue, silk carpets that covered the floor, and jars of honey hanging from the vines, inside. I smiled, as it was good to be home, where the scent of lilacs surrounded the hut.

"Next time don't be out so late!" Grapefruit said grabbing me by the ear. I laughed, "Oh, alright." I then turned to Ruby and Ryuu. "Make yourselves at home... really don't worry about anything," I said, waving my wings, as I walked off. I felt talons grab my wing, and I turned to see Ryuu, with a skeptical look.

How come you *seem* like you came from the Abandoned Kingdom, but you live with this, Grapefruit, in the Jungle kingdom?" they asked. "Oh! I forgot to tell you... my parents didn't want me, since they didn't have any powers, and I did. To them, I seemed like a freak... a shame to be around. So, they left me... and Grapefruit found me, and took me in."

Ryuu seemed content with my response and went over to have a little talk with Grapefruit. I sighed, and flopped onto my moss bed, in my room, glad to be home. I lifted my strong pearl necklace off my neck and laid it down. Suddenly, thoughts of all the other gryphons, I'd encountered, invaded my head. Okay, you need to learn how to deal with this, I told myself, taking a deep breath.

I tried to clear out the extra voices, to listen to my own; no... there's just too many. "Augh!" I let out a yowl, and the voices began to break. But I didn't have enough energy to reach my necklace now. "Need... to... stop… the… voices." I said, while stretching my talons out, managing to lift the necklace back on, and a sigh of relief escaped my lungs.

I could hear Grapefruit and Ryuu talking now. I walked out of my room, to see Ryuu laughing and Grapefruit saying, "If you're hungry just ask!" shoving a bowl of pears over to Ryuu. Ruby and I came to eat with Ryuu, "Hey guys I know we just met but I want to show you someone," I said smiling. "Darklight!!!" I called, grinning, and a tiny gryphonnet came running in, smiling. She was a gryphon-hybrid, as well. She had dark black feathers and purple under feathers, with bright round eyes, the color of lilacs, with a big smile crossing her face, "Yeah Noirscales? Oh pears!" she replied happily, jumping up to reach a pear and chomping down on it, like she was hunting a pig. "Hey Ryuu, Ruby, want to come with me? I asked, looking at them, while holding a pear in my talons. I'm going over to the mountains, because the best strawberries grow there." They both nodded. Ryuu and I, both, tied cloths, as open bags around our necks. "How do you tie this, it's just a piece of cloth?!" Ruby exclaimed. Grapefruit walked over and tied it into a bag around her neck. "There, not too hard," she commented, smiling sweetly to us all, and she waved us off. As we were in the air, flying on the wind, I caught a wind current, and did a spin in the air, laughing, enjoying myself. Ryuu seemed to spot the strawberries before I did, but stopped in midair. I dived under to catch them, before they fell. "What's wrong?" I asked, but they just froze, giving Ruby and I a terrified look. We exchanged glances and knew something was going on, so, without a word, we flew down, landing behind a rock, while I took a look over.

Down by the strawberries, lay a rotting, crimson-orange gryphon corpse; the feathers were pale in color, and the neck was sliced open... the eyes rolled back. "No... no, no... no, no, no..." I repeated, staring, in terror, at the body. Blood still dripped from the strawberry bushes, around the body. "What is it?!" Ruby inquired, sounding quite annoyed that we had to go hide.

I looked back at Ruby, my emotion, reflecting in my eyes, and Ruby's face, at once, changed. Ryuu was terrified, as he realized that the gryphon body, lying amongst the strawberries, was definitely murdered, clearly, beheaded by a mysterious enemy. The blood was fresh, with a strong metal smell. He neared it. "What happened here?" Ryuu asked, whilst whispering, as if someone unwanted would have heard. "I don't know... wait, I can hear someone. Stop talking," I whispered back, lowering my head to listen.

Chapter Two

<u>Fear Lies Ahead</u>

A deep voice was talking but I couldn't make out quite what they were saying. I felt a piercing, in my spine, as I turned to see a pair of emerald eyes, staring at me, mercilessly, and the figure of another gryphon slowly appeared, under the shadow of the mountains... the shadows, however, saving their identity. "

"Run!" Ruby screeched, shoving us aside and leaping forwards, extending her talons, with wings stretched out. Ruby landed on top of the figure, and they wretched in battle, blood flying. Ruby ended up on top and let out a roar, while stomping her talon down, one final time, on the enemy's head and raking some severe wounds. The figure managed to grab Ruby by the legs and flip her over, then flew away. However, Ruby lunged upward, grabbing him by his tail, and pulled him into the sunlight... it was a gryphon, from a neighboring kingdom. She slit his neck. Ryuu and I stared, in horror, at the gryphon, now lying dead on the ground. I looked up to notice heavy hatred in Ruby's eyes, "I know that Night Gryphon," she hissed, "…he killed my best friend." She was staring down at his corpse, then kicking him out of her way, she held up her talons to stare at the blood. "Ruby. Are you okay?" I asked, reaching out. She swatted my talons away. "I'm okay" she responded, staring off into the distance.

Suddenly, a local gryphon came running out from a cave, between the mountains, "That gryphon is Prince Thorn! The only heir to the Desert Kingdom!" pointing to the body in the strawberry patch. "Why have you done this? You have most certainly started a war!" the gryphon cried, turning to fly away. "Shame on all of you!" they yelled, as they flew off.

We stared at each other, in shock... we were now killers; and no one would believe that we are not evil, so, we all knew what to do. Run... we need to disappear and become something we're not, and we need to leave, now.

"Guys, I know somewhere we can hide for now; the Abandoned Kingdom - not many gryphons, nowadays, know where it is... but I was raised there, before I came to live with Grapefruit, in the Jungle. Only like four or five gryphons live there, now, so I'll be able to sneak you guys in," I suggested.

They both looked over at me. "Well there is nowhere else we can go," Ruby shrugged, then raised her head with a determined look. "Let's do it!" We looked at each other, then set off on our newfound journey, never to return home, until after the war had been fought.

"A storm is on its way," Ryuu commented, sniffing the air, as we flew. I looked up to see clouds beginning to gather. "We should find some shelter, we'll be at the kingdom tomorrow," I said. We built a fire, and it danced in the breeze. Ruby arrived, carrying a banana, some grapes, and a cow. We ate, then I sighed, as the stars stretched across the sky, "Well guys, we'll head off in the morning... I'm gonna get some sleep."

Ryuu and Ruby nodded, as I headed into the cave; where we had stopped, on a cliff over-looking the Ice Kingdom. Ryuu stayed outside, as Ruby walked in, and joined me. As soon as Ruby made a comfortable nest, she asked me a question, I wished she had never asked.. "Why did you suggest we go to the Abandoned Kingdom first?" I gave her a glare, impatience, getting the best of me... "I'll just get some sleep, and you can tell me in the morning," Ruby said. She yawned, stretching out her wings and talons, then curling up, falling asleep quickly.

"Morning'!" a voice said, in my ears. I opened my eyes to see Ryuu bent down, looking me straight in the eye. I sighed, and lifted myself up, onto my talons. The corner of my eye, noticed Ruby, stretching her wings ready to set off again. "We'll reach the kingdom by nightfall, if we don't stop on the way," I said, as I walked up beside Ruby and Ryuu.

Ruby turned to look at me, her red eyes, shining in the morning light, "Right... off we go then." I nodded, and the three of us set off, the wind, easily, carrying our wings. Trees passed below us, as birds flew by and, then, we heard a sudden roar in the distance. I turned to see the neighboring Desert Kingdom's forces, screaming and yelling at *our* kingdom's forces.

"I need to help!" Ryuu yelped, but I grabbed him by the tail, "You can't..." I told him. The guards could take you! We need to get somewhere safe." Ryuu seemed to understand and stopped fighting back, we continued on our path to the Abandoned Kingdom.

As the sun set, we paused, by a large boulder. "The Kingdom is behind this," I stated, as a matter of fact. Ryuu walked over to it and inspected it. "Er... umm, it... the Kingdom is... behind a rock? " He asked, clearly confused. I rolled my eyes, thinking, did this gryphon know anything? "The Abandoned Kingdom is only accessible through an animus-touched tunnel, inside the kingdom. You should know this, didn't you say you are helping rebuild the forest?" He looked down shyly.

"I guess so." I walked over and placed my talons up against the large stone. Ruby echoed the pattern. Together we threw our weight into the boulder.

At first, it didn't move, but then,-*creek*... the boulder slowly rolled away, gaining speed, as it went. Finally, the tunnel was open. "Follow me" I said, looking back, as they crawled through the tunnel behind me. The hard, familiar rock walls felt somewhat *comforting* to me. Then, the walls flew upwards into an open space, I caught myself with my wings, as I took a step out of the tunnel.

I looked, and over the horizon, I saw the mountains that I used to fly over every morning with my friends, laughing, talking, and hunting goats and sheep. Those memories flooded my mind, until a new voice entered. "Noirscales?" it said. " I need to find him... need to find my son. .Maybe, someday, he'll come home," it mumbled.

Chills crawled down my spine as I brushed off the voice of some nearby gryphon. Maybe, some other gryphon just had the same name as me. "Come on guys, this way!" I said. We flew across the mountains, the Kingdom, coming into sight, it looked old and ragged, but, it was home. I led the others down; and our talons landed on the rock hard ground.

"Rawrr!" Ryuu looked over, in a panic. "I think I heard a gryphonnet!" he exclaimed. Then, we saw a gryphon egg, hatching, under the full moon. The newborn gryphonnet had dark, black feathers, with silver 'eyes' on the tips, and white under its scales. Suddenly, we saw a huge, tiger-like animal, pounce and kill the baby gryphonnet, taking it away, as food. We stared, in shock, as the little gryphonnet's body dangled from the tiger-creature's mouth. Ryuu and I looked at each other, sharing the same fright. "Come on," I said softly, leading them to the knights' training room.

Most of the building was still intact, and the armor and weapons still hung from the wall... I walked over to the shields and brushed off some webs and dirt, and the shield shined in the light of the night sky.

"We can rest in the chambers tonight, and decide what to do tomorrow," I said, as my back turned on my friends, holding firm, the shield in my talons. Ruby walked up reaching her talon out to me. I looked back, "come on this way," I responded, and led Ruby and Ryuu through the palace. Her bright feathers stood out, like a scavenger in a sheep herd.

Ryuu's feathers began to fade to an emerald-green, as we passed by numerous gryphon skeletons, plastered against the hard stone cold walls. "It was a tradition, if a gryphon soldier died at war... I explained, their skeleton would be plastered to the wall, holding their spear, to ensure they can still serve in the afterlife." Ryuu seemed to calm down after that explanation. Ruby gagged, "What kind of tradition is that? You're basically *tying* your dead loved ones, to a wall, against their will!" I chose to ignore Ruby's comment.

Then, there before us, stood two tall wooden doors, with two gryphons fighting, carved on the door, with golden trim. I shoved the doors open, and as the cobwebs separated; they slid apart, on the wooden floor, leaving lines in the dust. I rested my talons on the floor.

"I'm sorry you've been through so much damage, Ruby," I said, as I looked back up. Ruby and Ryuu followed me into the corridors, where the chambers lie. The room was wide, with bookshelves on the left side and beds on the right... desks were evenly placed, by the bookshelves, with dusty carpets, lining the floor, leading up to the balcony, where you could look at the stars, stretching across the night sky. I sighed, happy that I was finally home.

The comfort of the stars, calmed me. I turned to see Ruby excited, checking out the weapons held on the walls. She took a katana in her talons and smiled at it proudly, probably, recalling some past battle. Ryuu was laid out on one of the beds, exhausted; he had his nose shoved in books, as he laid there.

"Goodnight, my friends," I said, walking over to one of the beds. I felt relief as I laid on the bed. The killing of the gryphons by the strawberries played on replay in my mind, "what if we can never go home?" I asked myself. I know I technically am *from* this kingdom but my home is in the jungle, now, and I just don't know. What if we die before we can return? Worry was getting the best of me, no... that's not true. We will go home. The war won't start, and we'll be fine... or so, I thought. I closed my eyes, as the darkness of sleep drifted over me.

Chapter Three

An Awaiting Cell

Noirscales! Noirscales!" a voice yelled, directly into my ears, talons shaking me awake. "What!?" I snapped, angry that I had been awakened, from my slumber. Ryuu was shaking head to toe. "What happened?!" I asked, taking Ryuu's talons in mine, comforting him. "It's Ruby…a gryphon from the Night Kingdom took her… she hasn't been back since morning," Ryuu said, his voice shaking. I could feel the fear invading Ryuu's mind. "It's gonna be okay, Ryuu... Ruby is strong," I reassured him.

I knew Ryuu could see doubt in my eyes, but I had to be strong, for *both* of them. "Wait here. I'll go look for Ruby, I'm sure she's okay," I said, letting go of Ryuu's talons, lifting myself up, onto the current of the wind. "Stay here," I said, turning my back to Ryuu, as I lifted off the balcony, into the horizon. I searched the land, as I hovered over the grassy meadows. Just then a very slight movement caught my eye. That could be Ruby! I thought to myself, diving down to get a closer look. My talons landed on the soft grass, and I crouched behind a rock, just close enough to hear what was being said. "You! It was you! You killed the gryphon prince!" a random, female voice screeched, with grief and hatred.

"No - please - I didn't, we just *found* his body... I didn't kill him!" Ruby's voice insisted, with slight fear. The other voice scoffed, "Yeah, sure, I know that..." Then it laughed, "*I killed* him, but thank god, *you* took the blame, you stupid jungle-loving gryphon!"

The two strange gryphons laughed and seemed to be enjoying their perceived victory. "No one will *ever* believe you, if you tell, that I killed him. Hah! You don't even know who I am," it snidely remarked.

I peeked out to see them... the female Night Gryphon was holding Ruby down on the grass, like she was going to kill her! "NO!" I yelled, leaping out from behind the rock, tackling her from on top of Ruby.

"You are not killing my best friend!" I yelled, in her face, now holding *her* down on the grass with *my* talons. She didn't seem the least bit scared, though. "Hah! You think you can threaten me?! You should *respect* me... Noirscales," she growled.

Wait, how does she know my name? Questions invaded my head, distracting me from holding her down, and she easily escaped my grip. "You *should* know me, as Queen Bluemoon, formerly, of the Abandoned Kingdom... now Queen of the Night Kingdom!" she snarled, "You're Noirscales, my *son*!"

Then, she hissed, "So, listen to your Queen, and let me dispose of your friend here, or be known as the gryphon who killed his own queen to save a dumb jungle-loving, fruit-eating gryphon."

I looked over at Ruby, knowing exactly what I had to do. "Ruby, run! I've got this!" I yelled, as I pounced on the queen, who was claiming to be my mother, pinning her down on the grass. I bent down to whisper in her ear, "I won't kill you," I growled, "but I will leave something for you to remember us by," and raising one talon, in the air, and throwing it down, as hard as I could, clawing through her eyes, I blinded her.

Screams of agony, then, filled the silence. "I can't see! I can't see!" the defeated queen cried, holding her face in her talons. I stepped off of her, scoffing, "Come on Ruby, let's go back. We need to figure out what to do about this upcoming war *and* the dead gryphon prince," I said, leading Ruby back to the balcony of the chambers.

"So… you're the prince of the Abandoned Kingdom?" Ruby asked, with a look of utter shock and confusion on her face. I shrugged, "*Apparently.*" "Hey! "You're back!" Ryuu called out, pulling Ruby and I, together, into a tight hug. We all laughed, full of joy to be with each other. "Alright guys," I said, "we need to start figuring out what to do about all of this," gesturing to the whole room. "About that, um," Ryuu commented, pulling out a scroll he'd found, "This appears to have everything we need."

The scroll had an instruction guide to Abandoned Gryphon obsidian armor. "Armor?" I asked, looking at Ryuu, "No, not that," he said. "Look at the note in the left corner." I looked down, and sure enough, there was a note. It read, "Here is the armor implant, you asked for, my Queen... the prince is on his way to the *Ice Kingdom* - meet him in the mountains. Then you'll be able to get the job done." My face lit up. "This is all the evidence we need!" I exclaimed, putting the scroll in the pouch, on my neck. I smiled.

"So, okay... now, how do we explain to our tribes that we aren't the killers of the prince?" Ruby asked, lifting her head. "That's a good point," I admitted. "We were the only gryphons, alive, that were by the body."

"We can figure that out when get there," Ryuu said, lifting himself up, onto his talons. I nodded, in agreement. "I'll go to the library and hopefully find more evidence... you two can go train, in the training room, in case we do have to battle." Ruby rushed off, with Ryuu at her tail. I spread my wings and headed for the library.

The library was lined with bookshelves, packed with books, wall to wall, most of the books, old and covered in cobwebs. Lights hung from the ceiling, reflecting on the windows. A beam of sunshine spread across the library, lighting up the room. The floor had huge rugs, maroon in color, with the designs of the starlit sky in silver trim.

"Looking for something?" an old, sweet voice asked. I turned, to see the librarian. She was incredibly old and frail... I couldn't help but notice, as her glasses hung over her nostrils. Her green eyes seemed to smile in the sunlight. "You young gryphons are very sweet," she said. I smiled at her complement. "Do you happen to know where battle planning books, and royal letters, are kept? I am the prince, so I have access," I said, bending down, close, so she could hear me. "Of course," she said, smiling, as she rambled over to a set of big doors. She held out a golden key and unlocked the lock. The doors slid open, leading into a dark and dreary room, where old, ragged scrolls and books covered the floor .

A wretched smell, suddenly, filled the air, "what's going on?" I asked, as I looked around for the librarian. She was gone. Then, I felt something cold and wet fall, limp, against my body. I looked, to see the librarian's dead body slumped over, against my side. Her neck had been slit, wide open, and blood was rushing out, like a waterfall... her eyes rolled back, showing no signs of life.

Agh!" I yelped, leaping away from the dead body. I need to focus and find the letter, I told myself. I began to notice what I thought was decorative ruby-colored splatters and head sculptures. The splatters were actually dried blood, I noted, as the light shined upon them. I began to notice the sculptures were actually various gryphon heads, plastered to the wall. There was one for each opposing tribe, with their eyes rolled back, and spears through their heads. I shuddered in disgust, I can't do this! I thought to myself, as I ran out of that nightmare of a library. After a while, Ruby and Ryuu returned to the chambers.

The dead body of the librarian, and the plastered heads, I was still seeing in my mind... it wouldn't go away. I could hear their voices, as if they were still alive, blaming *me* for their deaths. I clutched my head in my talons, letting out an ear-splitting scream of agony - why have I been cursed?! I wondered, and welcomed Ruby and Ryuu, as they entered the room.

How was training?" I asked them; Ruby and Ryuu smiled, "Really good... they have very effective weapons!" Ruby responded, as she patted Ryuu on the head, smiling. I smiled back. "Come on... you guys look hungry, and I have some pineapples." Ryuu looked eager and ran over to grab some. Ruby and I laughed, as we followed Ryuu.

"Are you okay," Ruby asked, noticing how shaken I was, "you seem a bit off?" "Oh, I'm fine, just a bit tired," I said, smiling. Ruby didn't seem to believe me, but stopped pestering me. Ryuu ran up and smiled, handing us some pineapples. "Come on, they are great!" Ryuu pulled us over and we fell on the floor, laughing. A scroll fell off the shelf with a big thump! "I'll go look at it" I said, patting Ruby and Ryuu's head, then standing up. Suddenly, I heard a booming voice, right behind us.

"Grab them!" the voice yelled. Talons suddenly grabbed us, pinning us all to the ground. Ryuu's screams and struggles broke me to the bone. Ruby lashed and yelled. I looked up to see the guard, who was holding *me* down. I was shocked. It was a Jungle Gryphon! Grapefruit was with the group, looking guilty. Did she rat us out as killers, I wondered... I forgot she follows me, every time I go to the mountains. She must've thought that *we* killed the prince! "We didn't kill him!" I yelled. "My *mother* did... Queen Bluemoon! Please, I can help you find her!" I pleaded, hoping these gryphons would believe me. "We know your lying.." they replied, "Grapefruit saw you by the body, and told us," the Queen of the Desert Gryphons, calmly, responded.

I knew it was hopeless to fight back. So, I stopped struggling and let the guards drag me out of the chambers, with my head hung low. It felt hopeless. This is our life now, I thought to myself. "Come on!" the guard yelled, forcing me to fly with them, to the Desert Kingdom, rounding us up, like sheep, surrounded and blocked off, at every possible escape. I sighed, and flew with the wind.

An hour passed like seconds, until we were thrown into jail. "I'll decide what to do with you later," the Desert Gryphon queen hissed, as she was walking away. The guards stayed behind to guard our cell.

I turned back, and saw Ryuu was still unconscious, on the floor, with Ruby. I should let them sleep , I said to myself, sighing and looking out the small window.

I saw young gryphonnets, playing, happily, in the sand. I felt a sudden feeling of jealousy creep up on me. "How dare those wretched gryphons! They must have *sand* in their *brain* to be this stupid!" I yelled, throwing a rock into a wall, then *shooting* fire at it.

"Clam down," Ryuu said, blinking his eyes open. Ruby, waking, turned to him, resting her head on his shoulders. Ryuu wrapped his wings around Ruby. "We'll be okay, I promise" he said, looking out at the guards. "We need to find a way out," I said, walking over to Ruby and Ryuu. They nodded.

Suddenly, we heard a new voice and looked over to see a senior guard, sending the others away. "Go! Useless lizards!" she shouted, as they flew off, heads hung low. She looked around, as if worried, and quickly headed over to our cell. "I know you didn't kill the prince..." she said. "I can get you out of here. Just wait for a little while," she whispered. "We have to wait for the queen to leave." We nodded, in understanding, and she rushed off. I turned around to Ruby and Ryuu. "How can we trust a gryphon, from the Desert Kingdom?!" Ruby growled, a new sense of betrayal, obvious in her eyes. "I don't know exactly what happened in your past, Ruby, but I think trusting this commander is our only option, for getting out of here!" I yelled back. Later, Ruby, Ryuu and I devised a plan, but we knew we had to wait until the queen left the village, before we could get our plan into action.

Days turned into weeks, weeks turned into months and the queen still hadn't left. "It's hopeless!" Ruby yelled, slamming her talons into the wall. I walked over to Ruby. "I understand your anger, Ruby, but we have to be patient, the queen *will* leave soon," I said, with sheer confidence behind my voice. Ruby looked up at me, her eyes red with tears. "We've waited four months! We are starving!" she yelled, extending her talons and leaping on me, holding me down. "You must be so stupid to think that we're gonna get out of here!" she yelled, her voice, choking. A sigh escaped Ruby 's lungs, as she let me go, and walked over to the opposite side of the cell. Ryuu joined her, and they laid next to each other, drifting off to sleep. I sighed, watching the clouds, as they passed by.

Chapter Four

Unsecured Safety

What now? I asked myself, looking down at Ruby and Ryuu. I have to figure out how to keep them safe, but what do I do now? The question kept repeating in my head, as if constantly playing on loop. I need to be strong for Ruby and Ryuu, I thought, looking down at them, peacefully asleep.

"It's time," a voice said, behind me. I turned around and saw the commander. "Really?! Ok... I'll wake them up!" I poked at Ruby. She blinked open her eyes, annoyed to be woken from her sleep. "It's time, get Ryuu up," I said, bending down smiling. Ruby understood and poked at Ryuu's' neck, till he got up.

We walked over to the bars, with the commander on the other side, waiting patiently. "Alright," she said, "the queen has just left the village and she took her guards with her. I told her I would stay behind to watch over the prisoners. I need you to stay as quiet as you can because we're going to sneak out right now" she whispered, while unlocking the cell door.

We looked left and right, not a gryphon in sight. "This way," her quiet voice whispered, as we moved through the tall, stoney palace. The moon shone through the windows, lighting up the patterns on the wall. "I know it's beautiful, right? I'm Sky, by the way," the commander said, smiling back at us, as we flew through the halls, passing beautiful sculptures, patterns and more. I stared, in awe, at all the beauty. "Up here" Sky said, from the front, taking a sharp upturn.

We followed as she flew through an open sky light, leading us into the firmament. Sky spread her wings out, smiling, taking in the air. "Okay, fly South and keep going, until you end up in the Gryphon Fins' village, then you'll be safe," Sky said. She handed me a magic scroll. "I have one as well," she said, "anything you write will show up on mine... if you ever need help, let me know." Sky waved us off, as she dove back down into the skylight.

Ruby and Ryuu followed me, at my tail, as we headed South. The wind brushed against our wings, as we flew against the strong current. None of us spoke a word, as we started our journey... we knew where we had to go. Hours passed, and then the Jungle Gryphon village came into sight. I knew the first thing we had to do was confront Grapefruit. We flew through the complicated maze of trees, and vines in the way, and I saw Grapefruit's hut. I immediately landed and slammed on the door, till she answered.

"What are you doing here?!" she snapped, but, before she could finish, Darklight shoved past her and tackled me, with the most vicious hug. "Where have you been, Noirscales? I missed you!" she whined. But, before I could respond, Grapefruit pulled her away. "He's a killer," she said, "he killed Prince Thorn of the

Desert Gryphons," she continued, looking into Darklight's eyes, emotionless. Darklight turned to Grapefruit, raging with anger. "I don't care! I don't care what you say, whether it is true or not... he's my brother! So we are leaving!" she screamed, and slapped Grapefruit with her tail as she turned to me.

Grapefruit scoffed and closed the door right after Darklight stepped out. "Did you kill him?" she asked, genuinely curious. "No, we were framed, by someone," I answered, coldly, staring out at the mountains. Darklight hugged me, "I don't care what others think, you're still my brother," she said. I smiled, and patted Darklight on the head. Then Ruby and Ryuu walked up behind us. "What now?" I asked, and Ryuu smiled. "Let's visit the Queen, and see if we can get her army on our side."

We all agreed, and flew past the vines, the platforms, the trees, and sloths. After some time, we landed at the entrance of the Jungle Queen's meeting-hut. It had a big chair, lined with roses, lilacs, and poppies.

The queen had bright, purple feathers, and violet eyes. A flower crown, lined her head, along with an arrangement of crystal-white spikes. Her talons were dark black, with lighter tones, under her scales. "What do you need?" she asked, letting her wings down, and tossing her head back, to look us in the eyes. "We need your support in battle, your majesty," Ryuu responded, calmly, bowing down to her. Ruby, and I joined him. The queen looked down, questioning our sincerity, but when she looked in Ryuu's eyes, she couldn't help but agree. "I will meet you at the middle platform, tomorrow morning, to discuss this," she said. Her voice sounded commanding. I turned to Ryuu; and I could see his fear of the queen. "Let's go guys," I said, calmly.

So, we headed out... the scent of the lilac flowers, surrounding the queens platform, soon fading. As we flew off, past the trees, for once, I felt at peace... as if I could, finally, let all of my struggle part. I smiled, swirling around in the air, letting go, at least for the moment. "Over here!" Ryuu called out, ahead of us, dipping down to a hut.

This one was decorated with vines, growing all along the walls, and beautiful roses, which bloomed upon the vines. The hut smelled like honey. Ryuu opened the door and led us inside. Ryuu fell down onto one of the chairs exhausted. You guys take what you want, I'm going to sleep," Ryuu groaned, slumping down into the chair. Ruby smiled, and sat down by Ryuu, letting him rest his head on her lap.

I walked over and tucked Darklight into a bed. Soon, everyone was asleep, except me. I laid on my bed, as the hours passed by. I was restless. My brain was endlessly thinking... What do I do now? What will happen next? I shrugged off the thoughts and shoved my head into my arms. I need to go to sleep, I told myself, sighing and rolling over. Why is this night taking forever? Why can't tomorrow just be here yet?

Wake up!" A voice called, from the other side of the room. I opened my eyes. The light was shining through the open windows. "It's time!" Darklight yelled, into the morning. "I'm on my way" I laughed, lifting myself off my talons. Ruby threw open the leaf curtains at the entrance of the room. "Come on! The queen is waiting!" Ruby called, practically dragging me out.

We raced across the tall trees, jumping from platform to platform, landing, swiftly onto the middle platform. Ruby paused, for a moment, letting me catch the view. The bright sun shone down onto the wood, the lines in the wood were dark and spinning, the colorful plants glowed, an aurora shone in the air all around us, like rainbows in the sky. Birds passed by, cheerfully chirping, and tweeting to each other.

"Oh, hello" a voice said. I turned to see the queen, sitting, with leaves covering her, to protect her from the blazing sun. A sweet smile appeared in her expression, as she greeted us. "Shall we begin?" she asked, smiling, Then, she led us to the edge of the platform and opened the leafy curtains, to show rows of her army, with armor, awaiting her orders and wisdom. I stared in awe, realizing she had done this, for us? I looked her in the eyes and it seemed as if she could read my mind.

No need to thank me," she replied... it is the least I could do. Now we need to strategize," her mood changing to serious. I nodded and walked upon the edge, looking down on the rows of the soldier gryphons below us. "My friends!" the queen started, with elegance. "I know we can win! We can stop this false war, and capture the real murderer of the Desert Prince!"

The Army roared with agreement and support. She stepped back, signaling to me, that it was time for me to speak. I dragged Darklight, Ryuu and Ruby up with me, "I promise that we will lead you to victory!" I said, raising my talons in the air, as my friends mimicked me. "Yeah!" the army roared, copying my "fist action."

I looked up at the sky. We will win. I know it, I thought, as I turned to Ruby. "You and Ryuu, keep Darklight with you, and make a plan with the queen.

I'll go try to find some help with the books in the library." I said to Ruby, who smiled, and responded with nodding. She headed over to the queen, with Ryuu and Darklight at her tail. I sighed, watching them go, as they talked with the queen. I looked back, one last time, before taking off into the sunlit sky. I headed to the library. Just then, somebody grabbed me by my tail, yanking me back. "Uhg!" I screeched, hitting the hard wood of the platform with a thud.

I turned around to see it was Ruby. "Don't go," she said, "the queen wants to talk with you." she smiled and stepped aside, letting me stand up. I wanted so badly to tell Ruby not to yank me by my tail, but I wanted to be professional, for the queen, so I shot an angry glare at Ruby, before turning to talk with the queen.

"So, Noirscales, Grapefruit did tell me what she saw, but I did not believe her. Seems I was right, but I did make a promise to watch over you." The queen seemed to look at me with a motherly expression, shining in her eyes. "I know you can do this. I promise you, we will be fine... you will lead us, brightly, into the future, and we will talk with the Desert Gryphons to convince them, and we will get rid of the conniving Night Gryphons, once and for all." The queen seemed sincere, as she said those words, her eyes, locking with mine. I nodded, knowing what I had to do.

"In order to find the real enemy, and help the Desert Gryphons, we must visit their palace tomorrow," the queen said, returning to her queenly ordering voice. I looked, deep, into the queen's eyes. She is afraid… but, why? I wanted to ask her, but, when I opened my mouth no words came out.

"You should go and get some rest. We're going to the Desert Kingdom tomorrow," she told me. The fear in her eyes was obvious, but she spoke with such strong confidence, that it was hard to believe she was scared. I reluctantly obeyed, and flew off with Ruby, Darklight and Ryuu.

Trees were just a blur, as the sun shone down on the village, as we flew. It seemed like a long journey, but, soon enough, we arrived at Ryuu's hut; Ruby, Ryuu, and Darklight all laid together, in an overly-huge, leaf hammock, laughing. It warmed my heart to see them like that.

"Surprise!" I yelped, leaping into the hammock with them. Ruby burst out laughing, and swatted me on my head, playfully. "You got me there!" Ruby chuckled, and turned back to cuddle into Ryuu. I shifted over and handed Darklight a peach. "Here in case you're hungry." Darklight looked up gratefully, and started munching down, on the peach. I smiled, and patted Darklight on the head.

Chapter Five

Promised Life

We all laid side by side to each other in the hammock, watching the night sky. Stars soared in the air like playful gryphonnets, laughing and play-fighting. I felt Darklight snuggle up close to me and I patted her on the head. She looked up at me, with her big violet eyes.

"Noirscales." she yawned. "Promise me you won't die, in the battle. I don't know what I'd do without my big brother." She looked up at me with the sweetest smile. "I promise, Darklight, I'll never leave you," I responded calmly. "Now get some sleep, Dark," I said, putting a soft flower underneath her head as a pillow. She yawned and drifted off to sleep.

I looked over and saw Ruby was asleep, cuddled up against Ryuu, who was still awake. "You shouldn't have promised your safety, to your sister... you don't know if you'll survive out there," Ryuu, plainly, said.

I could tell he was trying his best to save me from the pressure. We laid side to side staring up at the night sky, talking. "Yeah, but what would she do, if I told her, I didn't know if I'll survive or not? If any of us will survive?" I said, sighing, my breath drifting off into the night sky.

Ryuu looked over at me. "It's better than keeping her in the dark. Look, she cares about you. and since Grapefruit has turned on you, you are all she has left, so if you promise to stay alive, you better keep that promise!" He sounded very enthusiastic and confident. I could see it now... he was driving me to believe in myself! We held talons, in talons, and made a sacred promise that night.

"If we go down, then we go down together," and we knew we could do this. We knew that Ruby, Ryuu, and I, would return home alive, bringing peace along with us. That night, the journey had only begun. Morning arrived, like a bullet on a battlefield.

Within only a few hours we were in the air, with some gryphon guards, following us, to help protect us. The queen flew ahead, with us at her tail. Up ahead!" one of the guards yelled, which switched our focus to the front, the Desert Gryphon palace was coming into view. We have arrived! I could see Ruby and Ryuu beginning to look relieved. They're probably tired of flying, I thought to myself. We swayed downwards, and our talons hit the hot, burning sand. "Ouch!" Ryuu yelped, and Ruby laughed, "Did you not expect the desert to be hot?" Ruby asked Ryuu, playfully.

He looked a bit embarrassed, but quickly brushed it off, by reminding us why we were here. Quickly, we headed for the palace, the blazing sun following us, in our tracks. After what felt like forever, we were standing at the foot of the palace doors.

The Jungle Queen knocked on the doors, with no hesitation. She looked ready to stand her ground. A big gryphon answered the door. His feathers were a pale yellow, and he had a scar running from his face, across his body, to his tail. He must've been in some ugly fight. His blazing emerald eyes made it look as if he were staring into your soul. His frail was long and almost white, with hints of yellow. His talons and teeth were pitch black, along with his stinger. His feathers were white as snow.

"What do you want?" he asked, grumpily. "I want to see your queen... to speak with her, about the passing of her son," the Queen demanded. She gave the notice, she wasn't taking no for an answer. "Come on in," he said, "you can call me Anubis." He seemed quite unhappy with his job, as a guard; as he led us past long corridors, the walls lined with portraits of each queen and their king, from years past.

In the portraits, the queens and kings were lined with jewelry and crowns and flowers. The queens looked so friendly in all of the portraits, with their kings beside them, wearing silver armor, lined with golden trim, with their names in gold, along their armor.

"We're here," Anubis said, knocking me out of my

daze. I turned my head, to see long, tall, wooden doors, with cactus and vines surrounding them. Anubis shoved the doors open; and an olive-green carpet, with golden lines along the sides of it, led up the walls around the queen's room, while more cactus and vines hung from the ceiling, swaying in the wind, coming in from the skylight. I turned my attention to this gryphon queen, sitting upon a sliver throne. She had a golden crown, with a smaller, silver crown resting upon it... jewelry covered her neck, and silver earrings with an emerald gem, and golden piercings along her wings and wrists. She looked upon us with surprise.

"What brings you here, Queen Aloha?" the Desert Gryphon queen hissed, flicking her tail. "I've come here to correct this problem, the Jungle Queen said. "Noirscales, here, didn't kill your son... his *mother* did, the Queen of the Night Gryphons. I want your help..." she continued. "We need to combine our armies and finish *them* off." Queen Aloha spoke with such power that it would be foolish for the Desert Gryphon queen to deny. She huffed and looked around angrily. "Fine," she sighed, waving us off. "Meet me in between our kingdoms, on the border lake, in two hours." Queen Aloha nodded, and we bowed, before leaving.

Anubis led us back out of the palace, closing the door behind us, as we exited. A new light waited ahead of us only hours away. I reached out my talon, to feel the heat of the sun on my scales. I felt more talons rise beside mine. I noticed Queen Aloha had her talons in the air, next to me, smiling; a small bird landed on one of her talons, and she looked at it with absolute joy. "The world is pure beauty, isn't it?" she asked, watching the little bird. I had never been this close to royalty in my life. "Yeah... it's a true blessing,'' I agreed, looking over at the queen. She seemed so peaceful, and so happy.

It broke my heart to know we were going to war soon. "Noir scales," Queen Aloha said, turning to face me. I could see the sincereness in her eyes. "I've seen how you and Darklight no longer have anyone, but each other, and I care about you two. I promise you, if anything happens to you, during this war, I will care for Darklight, and give her the best life I can," taking my talons in hers. "I can't promise I will survive the battles, Queen Aloha, so thank you," I responded, smiling, brightly at her, as the sun shined down upon us.

She held my talons, then jumped forwards, and hugged me, taking me by surprise. I could see scarlet-white tears running down her cheeks. "Don't die! Live, you idiot!" she said, holding me in a tight hug. I wrapped my wings around her, too. How could a queen break down like this?

No, that doesn't matter... all that matters is comforting her, I told myself, trying not to seem scared, or worried, for Queen Aloha. After a few minutes, she contained herself, letting me go, and we flew over to the border, to meet the Desert Gryphon Queen. As she had promised, the queen was waiting, on a pile of rocks. She looked unhappy to be here. Probably wants to be back in her savannah, I thought, as we settled down, getting ready to talk. "I have my army ready for your command,

Aloha," she said, getting right to the point. Aloha nodded, and raised herself up onto the stones, with this other gryphon queen. "As I've already stated, the Desert Queen said, "I can promise you, we will protect you and your tribe, but we demand the same, in return, as well. I expect regular meetings to speak about this. I'm already planning an attack for tomorrow. We will fly over to the Night Kingdom, and attack, in the morning. This is not a question, this is an order... I'll see you then."

The Jungle Gryphon queen seemed bothered by her remark, but agreed, nonetheless. Little did she know, that would be a big mistake. We said goodbye and departed. The pressure of the battle tomorrow morning rained on us, like huge heavy weights.

The day passed by like seconds, and we found a place to rest for the night. Soon enough, we were in the air, awaiting a blood bath. The armies flew behind us, spears in hand, and armor on. The commander flew up, in the front, next to Queen Aloha and the Desert Gryphon queen, whose name was Amber. Her army flew beside the *Gryphon Fins,* whose help she had enlisted, and we followed right behind. Bloodshed was certain; we flew, tense, in the air, knowing, only moments from now, we would be facing other gryphons, talon to talon. Time passed, slowly, as we stood on the battlefield, awaiting orders from the Queens.

Queen Aloha, and Queen Amber, called me over. I approached, feeling all eyes on me, as I now stood beside royalty. "We want you to make the call to start the battle," Queen Aloha stated, as I arrived beside them. I stood, shocked, but knew that this was what I had to do. I simply smiled, nodded, and took off into the air. I turned to face our armies, Jungle Gryphon, Desert Gryphon, and Gryphon Fins, combined.

"We can do this! We are strong! For now we are united! We are one! Gryphon *Fins*, Desert and Jungle Gryphons, attack!" Moments after that, the bloodshed began. Gryphons raced across the field, tackling each other. I dove down, and ran, with the hard rocky ground, beating against my talons, as I raced across this battlefield.

A dark-blue gryphon tackled me, racking his spear sharp talons against my armor. Laughing, I reached out and pulled his mouth open. Shooting fire down his throat; he screamed in agony, as death gripped him by the neck, literally, stealing his life away. I turned and saw Ryuu, being held under a large gryphon's talons... by his neck, bloody scratches, which declined on his body.

"No!" I yelled , leaping over onto his attacker. A blind mad gryphon turned to face me. I noticed in a heartbeat that it was my mother, Queen Bluemoon... she still had the ugly scars on her face that crossed her eyes, showing her blindness. I leaped, reaching out my talons, but she swatted them away and pinned me against the ground. I yelped, as she shoved her teeth into my throat pain throbbed as I threw her off of me.

She scowled in pain as I racked my claws over the back of her neck. "I hate you!" I screamed, as I ripped out her throat. Her body went limp, falling to the ground and I began to tumble around in exhaustion.

Staring down at the, once alive, body of my supposed mother, I shivered. Ryuu threw his wings around me. I could hear the words "thank you," whispered, under his breath.

The battle raged around us, but I seemed to have lost control of my body. I wanted to scream. I wanted to escape, but all I could do was stare at my bloody talons, the very talons, that murdered my own kin.

Chapter Six

Bloodstained Talons

I looked up, and noticed a small gryphonnet, racing towards my mother's bloody corpse, tears streaming down its face, like a waterfall. "Mom!" the poor gryphonnet screamed, in agony and grief, throwing itself onto the corpse, hugging her tightly, and sobbing uncontrollably. Just then one of the Night Gryphons grabbed the gryphonnet, and flew off. I watched, then looked back down at the body. It started raining. The rain fell against the battlefield, as the bodies lay all over the hard, rocky ground, staining it red.

I had killed their queen... we won. I should be happy, but I couldn't get the thought of the sobbing gryphonnet out of my mind. Am I a villain? The question played on repeat in my head. I gripped my head, in my talons. "Noirscales, come on, it's time to go home," Ryuu said, pulling me to him. I looked at him, my eyes dry of emotion, and all I could do was nod and follow. We passed by the dead bodies of Night Gryphons, Desert Gryphons, Gryphon Fins, and Jungle Gryphons, each.

Just then my blood turned cold. A scarlet red body, lay on the ground, barely breathing, covered in blood and open wounds. Immediately I knew who it was. "Ruby!" Ryuu yelled, running, and falling down beside her. I rushed to his side, as he gripped Ruby's head, in his talons, holding her up. Ryuu's eyes teared up, and Ruby slid her talon up, against his cheek.

"Ryuu, don't cry," she said. "I never got the chance, but now it is good. I need to tell you… ,I love you." Her last breath exhaled, like a blown out candle. Ryuu screamed, up at the sky, as he pulled Ruby in close, hugging her. He seemed unable to accept her death. I knew I couldn't comfort him, so I just pulled him up.

"No! No! I can't leave her!" Ryuu yelled, but, I grabbed him by the tail. "Ryuu. she's gone," I said, firmly. As we headed back, neither of us spoke a word.

We approached the troops, as they were taking off, into the air, and Queen Aloha headed our way. "We thank you for helping us, Noirscales, and Ryuu," she said, pulling us into a hug.

Suddenly all my feelings came crashing back like a wave. I couldn't control myself as I fell into Aloha's wings, and sobbing screams, of grief, escaped my throat. Her comfortable sky blue wings held me tight, in the hug. She pulled me tighter, comforting me. "It's okay," she said, while holding me. Somehow, those two words comforted me, knowing that I had somebody's shoulder to cry on. Soon enough we headed back home.

The jungle looked exhausted, trees hung low, heavy with vines, in the swallow of this jungle. Jungle Gryphons flew around, talking and chatting, as normal. As soon as we reached the village, families reunited... gryphonnets ran into the army, to find their family members. Most gryphons laughed, and cried tears of joy, jumping into each other's arms.

As most of the army dispersed, we saw

gryphonnets and elders, together, near the dead bodies of friends and family, mourning their loss. Ryuu didn't speak to any gryphon as he passed through the trees, into his hut. I hesitated, watching him go.

"Leave him, he needs time... he'll come around, don't worry," a sweet old voice said, beside me. I turned to see a sweet, elder gryphon, her feathers, the colors of honeysuckles. She had light green eyes and dark gray horns and spikes. Her wings were a dark black-green, with golden splotches on the feathers. She gave off the vibe of a sweet, caring grandmother. She was wise, so I decided to listen.

"Every gryphon loses someone, at some point," she said. "Ryuu lost his mother, when he was just five years old... so he's not gonna take Ruby's death easily." My heart sank. Ryuu had always seemed so happy and bright, but he lost his mother, at such a young age. I stood up to go and talk to him but worry caught me by the throat. What if he doesn't want to talk and just wants to be alone?

I knew the elder could see my doubt, as I turned to face her. She smiled, nodding at Ryuu's hut. "Go, he needs you," she calmly said. I nodded. Those words were all I needed to hear.

I made my way to Ryuu's hut, dodging some trees and some sleeping gryphons, on the way. I stood in front of the door, and my mind raced with things to say. Ryuu opened the door; he looked miserable. He had baggy, bloodshot eyes, and he dropped his head low. I opened my arms, and Ryuu collapsed into my hug. I held him close for some time.

"Ryuu, do you think Ruby would want you to miss her? We will remember her, and she will be grateful, I promise you that," I whispered, resting Ryuu's head upon my shoulder, as he sobbed. "I think I can," Ryuu sniffed, and gathered himself together.

Days passed, and Ryuu stayed in his hut, only leaving to go get some berries, every couple of days. My worry for Ryuu grew stronger, by the day. A month passed, with the same cycle.

One day, I noticed Queen Aloha, knocking on Ryuu's hut door. I raced over, ready to talk *for* Ryuu. I was shocked to see the queen was crying. She stopped knocking, as I landed on his doorstep, beside her. She was holding a letter. Ryuu opened his door, looking like he hadn't slept in weeks... he looked horrid.

The queen sighed, handing him a letter, without saying a word. She leapt up, and dove into the nearest tree, heading up to the top. Ryuu took the letter and closed the door, once again, retreating into his dark hut.

I wondered if the queen was still there. I hopped up the tree, the bark feeling hard, underneath my talons. I then climbed up and laid down on the leaves, where I saw a beautiful gryphon, I'd never seen before. Her feathers were navy blue, with splotches of black. The tips of her wings were a beautiful, stark white and her face faded from a dark blue to a pearl white. She had dirt-brown eyes, like coffee, filled with caramel. Her spikes were a dark brown with a hint of white on the very tips. She looked like a goddess.

The beautiful gryphon noticed that she had caught my attention. "I've been seeing you around," she said... "come on over, people call me Pine." She waved her tail at me. We laid down next to each other, watching the stars above us, as they shimmered and fought in the night sky. "Look that one looks like a star," Pine commented, pointing at a combination of stars, and I laughed. "Yeah, it really does," I responded, happily, smiling at her. We looked up at the sky, again, and I began to notice some stars that looked like a smile. "Look the night's happy," I joked, pointing up at the smiling stars.

She elbowed me in the gut, laughing. I playfully kicked her, on the leg. Soon, the sky dimmed, and I knew it was time for me to go to bed. I flew down the tree, and into the dark, peaceful jungle floor, where most gryphons slept.

The whole jungle seemed as if it slept, as one. Sleeping gryphonnets twisted and turned, inside their huts. The night had an uneasy feel to it, as if the jungle was being watched. Gladly, I soon made it to my hut.

Darklight was already cuddled up in a pile of long leaf sleeves, fast asleep. I laughed and walked into my room. I fell onto my bed, in relief, glad to be home. Thoughts of Pine repeated, on that loop, in my mind. I smiled. God, she's just everything I need, I thought to myself.

Sleep came easier that night... as I closed my eyes and drifted off into slumber. The dark room consumed me, and words played out, on instinct, in my head.

"When Sea and Ice join the fight.
The truth will be brought into the light.
The heir of the moon shall soon return.
In a blaze of fire fate will turn.
When the day, war comes to end,
Some tribes will never again be friends.
The *royal* blood is called upon.
To save the peace we depend on,
But if they fail in this quest,
No gryphon, again, shall ever, rest."

Chapter Seven

<u>A Prophet Arrives</u>

The words played, over and over... what could this mean? I asked myself to reach out my talons, to the words, but they faded away. Soon, morning arrived, and birds sang, outside my hut. I sighed, in annoyance. Probably, just a bad dream, I told myself. Wait, no... it has to mean something. I walked up, into the middle room of the hut, and grabbed pears. My mind raced with questions. I should write it down. I reached for a scroll.

The paper was very delicate, so I carefully wrote down the words from my dream. "When Sea and Ice join the fight, the truth will be brought into the light. The heir of the moon shall soon return. In a blaze of fire, fate will turn. When the day, war comes end, some tribes will never again be friends. The royal blood is called upon, to save the peace, we depend on. .But if they fail, in this quest, no gryphon, again, shall ever, rest."

I mumbled to myself while scribbling away at the scroll. "Morning Noirs... whatcha writing?" Darklight asked, stumbling off her seat and walking towards me, with pears in hand. She offered me one, as we began to talk. "Okay, don't be scared, but, I don't think the war has fully ended; I'm going to head to Queen Aloha's palace, in a little," I said, grabbing the scroll. The ancient paper felt light in my talons. I was scared I'd rip it. Darklight clung to my arm. "Don't go fighting again, Noirscales! Don't get hurt!" she begged.

I bent down and looked her in the eyes. "Darklight, I'm doing this for your future. I don't want you to live in a destructive world... that's why I'm fighting, now, to make this world safe for you." Darklight threw her wings around me. "Ok, but don't be stupid, and get yourself killed... promise big bro?" she asked. I smiled and patted her on the head. "I promise."

A loud knock came from the front. I walked over, to see a gryphon outside my door, with the royal armor on, holding some kind of letter.

I quickly unlocked my door, not wanting to upset the guard. "Prince Ryuu wants to invite you to his crowning this evening," the guard said, handing me the letter. "Wait, prince?" I asked, but before I could finish, the guard had moved on to the next hut. Ryuu is a prince... of the Jungle Gryphons? No wonder Ryuu and Aloha look alike. I smiled, at the thought, laughing it off.

"Okay, Darklight, lets have fun at the crowning ceremony this afternoon, then I'll go show this prophecy, to the queen." Darklight smiled. Time passed, and as we approached noon, we made our way down to the crowd. I immediately found Pine. We sat together, Me. Pine, and my little sister, Darklight.

When Queen Aloha stepped onto the platform, in the auditorium, the whole crowd went silent, and she began to speak. "Today, we are gathered here, as one, for the crowning of my son, Ryuu," she smiled, raising her wing, for Ryuu to step up. He had golden rings around his neck and wrists. Ryuu smiled, and touched foreheads with the queen.

They then walked up in front of the crowd together. A golden crown with emerald lining in the pattern of vines. Gryphons, of the Jungle, roared Ryuu's name, in support, as the crown was placed upon his head. Then the party began.

Gryphons began to play drums and make music, dancing and laughing, crowding the jungle. Music flew in the air, while gryphon colors flashed in the sunlight. Pine flew up above the dancing gryphons and began to sing a song. She flew in circles, signing, talons open wide. A darker scaled gryphon, then, joined her, and they flew together, in the light of day, singing along to the music. They seemed to dance in sync with the music, as if it pulled them in a certain way.

Just then Pine pulled the other gryphon in for a kiss. At that moment my heart broke, Pine, it seemed, was already taken. It's fine, I thought to myself, as long as they are happy. Ryuu flew down ahead and began to chat with some of the other royals.

I supposed, I should go congratulate him, so I made my way past all the dancing gryphons, to his side. Ryuu stood by a table. He looked so sophisticated... he held a glass of water, while speaking with the others. "Why hello prince..." I jokingly said, as I greeted Ryuu, bowing my head, teasingly. Ryuu laughed and playfully kicked me in the leg. "I was going to tell you..." Ryuu started, rubbing the back of his head, in embarrassment.

We spent the rest of the night chatting away and enjoying the night, till sunrise. "Well I gotta go now," I said, waving at Ryuu, as me and Darklight started out. "Go on ahead, Darklight," I said, "I have to give the queen this letter." I turned back to the palace.

Darklight didn't question me, and simply, flew off through the dark forest, to our hut. I turned and faced the tall trees. As the sun creeped up, my breath began to shake. As I made my way through the forest, up to the royal hut, the light of the morning sun shone down on the forest, lighting up a small hole, underneath a tree.

It seemed to call me. You're curious. Do it.

Voices played, once again, on repeat, in my head. "No." I thought to myself, "I have to bring this letter to the queen." As I reached the palace-hut door, I could tell the queen was already asleep. As the flowers hung from her ceiling, they seemed to be sleeping themselves.

The whole forest breathed as one, under sapphire skies, along with dancing, morning stars. Thoughts of losing this home suddenly filled my head. I blocked them out, laying the letter, at the foot of the door. She will find it, I reassured myself, as I took off... my star-speckled wings, gracing over the leaves of the trees, as I flew. I returned home. The hut was quiet, as I made my way to my room, passing the hanging honeysuckles. A feeling of uneasiness creeped up my spine, as I closed my eyes, and drifted off to sleep.

"It's your fault!" I heard. "We died because of you!" the voices yelled. I stood alone, in a dark room... I opened my mouth to yell for help, but no sound came out. In front of me stood the librarian, Ruby, and the Desert Gryphons' heir.

No... no, no... it's not my fault! It can't be!" I yelled, inside my head, taking dream-steps back. They looked at me with pure hatred, covered in the wounds, which they had when they died. The heir stood in front of the others.

He looked down upon me, with utter disgust. "It is your fault, you know? Nothing would've happened, if you never left that cave, but you said, 'no, I'm going to help those other gryphons,' and look where that brought you,." he said, waving his talons around in the air, as he moved his head, trying not to look me in the eye. "You're the reason my friends *died*!" I shouted, by accident. The heir stopped in their pacing. A wicked smile crawled upon his face. "Let's talk about your friends... they didn't have to be here. You brought them here," he hissed, pacing towards me.

Fear creeped up to me, as he wrapped his tail around my neck, pushing me down, onto the ground. I hit the ground with a hard, painful thud. Spikes, from the heirs' tail, stabbed at my neck, threatening my life.

He bent down, his emerald-green eyes, locking with mine. "It is your fault, but *you're* still alive," he said softly. A sudden realization hit me, like a spear. They are trying to seize my weak spot to get me ready for the upcoming battle. I smiled calmly, and threw the heirs' tail away from my neck, though the scars from their tail, remained. I felt no pain, only fear.

"You all may have died, but you died before the war! The agony of watching your loved ones, taken from you... leaving your friend's corpse on a battlefield, you can't know! You died before other tribes couldn't even look you in the eye, because of your heritage!" I cried, screaming. "I'm not giving up! I WILL WIN THIS WAR and watch my sister grow up, and gryphons CELEBRATE!" I said, fighting back the pain."

I will win, so all future gryphons can live in a world of peace and hope! So my sister can be safe!" I yelled, smiling as tears ran down my face. Lifting my talons in the air, I yelled, "I'm not scared of you! None of you can stop me from saving this horrible world!"

The light beamed into my eyes as I woke from my slumber. I walked out to see Darklight, pacing back and forth, making markings on our wooden floor. "Are you okay?" I asked my sister, walking up and holding her in place. Just then I noticed the panic in her lilac eyes. "What's going on, are you okay?" I repeated more eagerly begging for an answer of reassurance. She looked at me, her eyes red from tears. "Look, outside..." she said, her voice trembling. As she pointed to the window. I looked back letting go of her talons as I cautiously walked over to the window lifting the leafy curtain.

I stood shocked as gryphons screamed and raced across the jungle carrying their little ones, who clung to their parents tears streaming, down their faces. Screams of agony coiled, in the jungle, as the jungle burned down. "Darklight, come on, follow me!" I said, picking her up and putting her on my back. "Hold onto my wings," I said, bracing myself for the fire to break through. "I'm gonna break the door down," I said, looking up at Darklight, who clung to me like a scared lizard.

I ran forwards, smashing the wooden door down, and leaping into the air. Smoke filled the space. "Cover your mouth and nose!" I said, yelling up at Darklight, hoping she wouldn't consume any smoke. Trees fell, spreading the fire, across the grassy jungle floor. Heat, beat against my wings, as I made my way past the fire. "Here I'll take her!" one of the guards said, flying up to me. I handed Darklight to the guard. "Where's the prince?" I asked, in alarm, and he looked somber.

"Trapped in the royal hut," the guard said, lowering his head; he wished me luck, rushing off with Darklight, towards the other gryphonnets. I nodded and turned to face the blazing forest. The fire was close to devouring the palace hut. "Ryuu! Call out to me!" I yelled, hoping Ryuu heard me. I heard a faint call, of my name. That sounds like Ryuu! I rushed to the palace. Pillars had fallen, fire and smoke filled the air. I rushed past the fire, and suddenly, a pillar crashed down beside me. "Augh!" I yelped, as it smashed my wing.

A throbbing pain drilled through my wing, as I pulled it out. Crap... my wings broken! It's fine. I can still find him! I told myself to run through the hut. Soon enough, I found Ryuu under a pile of pillars and sticks, that were partly on fire. "Ryuu!" I screamed, in shock, rushing to his side. "Noirscales! Get me out of here," Ryuu said, weakly, with a trembling breath.

I nodded, and began to hit the pillars. Small chips came off, one by one. Ugh, it's not working. I need to find some other way. I told myself, frantically, looking around. There! A rope! I rushed forwards and tied the rope onto the pillar.

"As soon as you feel loose enough to move, get out, alright?" I asked Ryuu, and he nodded, with a weak smile. I then tied the other end of the rope to me. You're strong, you can do this, I told myself, as I began to run forwards... a throbbing pain filled me, as the rope got tighter. "I won't give up!" I screamed, in pain, running faster. The pain became unbearable, I couldn't go any longer. Just then, I thought of Darklight.

Do this for Darklight, I told myself... just then I heard Ryuu yell that he had made it out. I sighed in relief, dropping to the floor.

Chapter Eight

<u>Champion Heart</u>

Get up, you have to get Ryuu out of here, I told myself, as I dragged him onto my back. With the rope, I secured Ryuu to my back. I took off and made my way back to the cliff, with the rest of the kingdom. I laid down and untied the ropes, letting Ryuu drop to the grassy ground. "Have the medics take a look at him," I said. "They ought to look at your wing, as well," the queen, said coming over, from my left. "Hello, your majesty." I greeted her, by bowing my head. I had ignored the horrible pain in my wing, while I was flying, but now it has become more noticeable. "Yeah." I said, wincing from the pain. "Is Darklight okay?" I asked. The queen smiled, "She's fine, Go. I know you need to see her," the queen said, stepping aside. I nodded my thanks and rushed over to where the gryphonnets were being watched, by the elders.

I noticed Darklight, in a corner, curled up asleep. I walked over and laid down beside her. Covering her with my good wing, I quickly fell asleep beside my little sister. Morning arrived early, as the sun shone in my eyes. I yawned, and smiled up at the welcoming sun. Darklight stretched and yawned, as she woke.

Darklight looked up at me, her bright curious lilac eyes beamed, with worry. "It's gonna be okay, Darklight. we can fix the forest," I said, turning down to nuzzle her. "Come on, let's get your wing fixed," Darklight said, standing up in full seriousness. I nodded, lifting myself up from the hard ground.

As we made our way past the camp gryphons had built on the grassy meadow, we noticed the healers rushing back and forth, between all the campsites, with hurt gryphons, and even carrying some to a medic camp site. Darklight called a healer over to us. She noticed my wing, as soon as she arrived and began to examine it.

"Looks like it's broken in two places and a few feathers are swaying around freely. We'd better get your wings fixed quickly," she said, adjusting her glasses, as she led me and Darklight to the medic camp site. As we entered, we noticed old and young gryphons laying on leaf beds, with medics around each of them, watching them, closely. The medic pointed to an empty leaf bed and ran to get her supplies. "I'll be fine," I said, smiling, as I walked up.

I noticed my leaf bed was right next to Ryuu's. He looked horrid, with huge, ugly scars, that ripped his feathers away, leaving only burnt skin, and a scar from his nose to right beside his eye. He was asleep, but looked like he was in horrible pain. One of his horns was broken, with chipped off feathers, but those *would* grow back soon. He is in pain, but he will be fine. He knows that he has to survive, and he doesn't give up too easily," a sweet old voice said.

I turned to see the wise elder, whom I had talked to *before* the forest burned down. She looked in the direction of the forest. "I've seen many fires in my lifetime, but this... it's not natural.

The heat of the fire and the effect it had on other gryphons, wasn't normal. Definitely Sky, Wing, Fire, or another hybrid." I was shocked by the elders' wise words but now that I think about it, the elder has a point. She could be right about this. "Ok I'll tell Ryuu, when he wakes up," I said. "No, you're talking to me first..." the queen said, as she neared my leaf bed, the letter in her talons. She seemed very bothered.

They probably already read the letter, I'm surprised it didn't burn in the fire. She let out a sigh of relief, as she sat down next to me. The queen being so close to me kind of soothed me, and she began to clean up my wing, while talking to me.

"So, Noirscales, it seems you were given a prophecy. Thank you for letting me know. I was able to find your message, in the lines that mentioned this forest. So, I had the guards on ready, to get the gryphonnets, and elders, out early," she said, while applying a cobweb cast to my wing. I smiled up at her, as she applied the final layer. "Also, thank you for saving my son," she said....

"I owe you a lot," before I could respond, she continued, "Alright, there, just keep it in that cast... you can still move it, just don't put much pressure on it," she said, as she was stepping away. I noticed that I could see all the joints of my wing, in a linked, cobweb cast, so I could still stretch my wing. I nodded, in thanks, and turned to leave... but someone grabbed my tail, and stopped me. I turned around to see it was Ryuu. "You're awake!" I exclaimed, falling down to hug him. He wrapped his wings around me, as a big smile spread across his face.

He said, "You saved my life, Noirscales, without even thinking of your own!" He was slow in letting me go, out of the hug. I nodded shyly, and shrugged... "Well, you're my best friend, Ryuu; I couldn't just let you burn in a fire." I could see, even though his body suffered many injuries, he looked happier than a gryphonnet, getting their first prey. It warmed my heart.

We talked for hours, but then, it was time for me to go look for Darklight. I said goodbye to Ryuu, and the Queen, before walking out.

I knew it was around noon, because the sun was in the middle of the sky, beaming light down on us, below. I noticed Darklight returning with some other gryphons, looking very proud. I ran over to greet them. "We did a patrol around the cliff," she said. "There are no intruders so far, and we did some hunting."

"We have some prey and lots of fruit," the gryphon in the front said, to the royal guard, who approached beside me. The gryphons bowed their heads and began to hand out food to all the weak gryphons and gryphonnets, first, then left the rest for the young fit gryphons like me.

I walked over to the pile of food, which they left in the middle of our camp. Let's see, oh they've got sheep! I began to tear down on a sheep. As Darklight joined me, she began to go on and on about everything she saw, while hunting with the older gryphons. "So we saw a big mound of dirt... then I tackled it, and there were sheep under it, so I killed the sheep, and I got five! FIVE!"

Darklight emphasized. Reacting to her tackling of the sheep, laughing and roaring, I chuckled. "I bet the sheep were petrified!" I joked, while enjoying the show. Darklight laughed, and laid down next to me, drifting off to sleep. I looked down at the sleeping gryphonnet, and a pain hung in my chest.

I need to keep her safe, but there is still a war knocking at our door, I thought to myself, pulling Darklight closer, and covering her with my good wing. "I promise to always be by your side," I whispered, while she was sleeping, nuzzled up under my wing . Ryuu appeared and laid down beside us. None of us spoke a word... and we covered each other with our wings, falling fast asleep.

I woke up to hooting owls, as they flew across the starlit sky. The others were still asleep, so I got up and looked down at the two of the, cuddled up. "Take care, my dears," I said, bending down and hugging each of them. Something seemed to be calling me to the burned down forest. Maybe I can find something about the prophecy there, I thought to myself, as I spread my wings, bracing myself for flight. I took off, shooting myself into the air.

As I got to the forest, I landed on the shriveled black, burnt ground, once green and thriving, with trees and leaves covering the forest floor. The smell of burnt trees filled the air, as I walked through the, now dead forest, the ground crunching under my talons. Soon, I came across the smell of blood. I ran forward, again, and noticed a dead Desert Gryphon and Sky Wing Gryphon, next to each other, with burn marks on their necks and backs. Of course! The elder was right!

I looked around, to make sure I would remember this spot. There were a few green leaves that marked the left of the area, with a few dead possums, who stank horribly, on the right, which would make this easy to find again. Just then, I noticed a spear plastered into the Sky Wing's head. It had cactus patterns on it with golden lining. Yep, that's a Desert Gryphon spear, I noted, looking around for any others. I gotta go get some guards to come clarify these gryphons' identities, I told myself, turning to leave.

Back at the campsite, the village gryphons were just starting to get up and go to get food. I turned to see Ryuu, waking up and yawing. I rushed over, with some peaches. "I've got breakfast! You two eat up, I'm gonna go visit the queen," I said, as I handed both of them a peach. Darklight sent me a thank you look, and Ryuu nodded, as the two sat together, talking and eating.

I knew I needed to tell Queen Aloha, what I had discovered, immediately. I headed towards the elder gryphons, gathered in the middle of the camp site, sharing their food, and talking about the current situation. "Ah! Noirscales, why don't you join us? You're very wise for a youngster..." one of the elders called.

I looked over. Honeysuckle, Grapefruit, Pomegranate, and Queen Aloha, were all gathered, there, too. So, I gladly accepted, and sat down to listen to the elders' wise words.

"I've never seen a fire burst out that suddenly before," Honeysuckle blurted out. Grapefruit nodded... he looked somber, as he turned his head to look at our once-happy, and thriving home, that was now ashes and dust. "Well, we can thank Noirscales, for us getting everyone out safely," Queen Aloha butted in... she looked around at the curious faces of Honeysuckle, Grapefruit and Pomegranate, before continuing.

"The night before, a letter from Noirscales was sitting on my doorstep... it was a prophecy. I was able to figure out the clues, pointing to this very event, so I got the guards on the ready, to rush everyone out of the forest." As Queen Aloha finished talking, she settled herself down, shooting me a proud glance and nod. I smiled, and looked around, as the elders began to ask me questions. . I paused, waiting for the questions to die down, before speaking. "Actually," I started, "I know who set the fire. Follow me."

I stood up and spread my wings. The queen shot up, after me, followed by the elders, and I led the way to the scene. We soon arrived by the bodies of the intruders. Grapefruit stepped forwards, bending down to examine the first dead gryphon... he lifted up the head of the gryphon, by the chin.

"Huh... I know who this is, or, who he *looks* like, anyway - his name is Thorn - he is part of the Desert Gryphons' royal family.   There *was* a twin brother, that disappeared years ago," he said. "This must be him." We stood, staring, bewildered... then, an unexpected gryphon came out from behind a pile of ash.

"That's my brother," he said... "you're wise, for a Jungle Gryphon," he added, as he stood there, looking almost identical to the dead gryphon, except for his eyes. "No!" I yelled, stepping back "You're dead!". I wished the ground would just open up and take me whole.   He laughed, and then, sighed, as he was looking down, at his brother. "No... that was my royal guard,, he died to protect me... I put on his armor, and gave him my royal jewelry, to make him look like me, so I could escape," he said calmly, picking at his talons, with his teeth.

He spit out a stick, then looked up at Queen Aloha, as if he just saw someone he loved, come back to life. "I've got an idea!" he said. "You shelter me, and we will keep going on with the fake news of me being dead, so I can live a normal life!" he exclaimed, happily, curling his talons in, as if he had just discovered the world's biggest secret. We exchanged glances at each other with weary looks. The queen swallowed down, her fear, and looked up with authority.

Chapter Nine

<u>Decisions of War</u>

I will leave this decision to Noirscales, because he's the reason we found you," Queen Aloha told the prince, sitting down with the other elders, while they all looked down at me, from the boulder they sat upon. All eyes are on me… I can do this, I sighed and stepped forward. "Following gryphon laws," I said, "because you stepped foot onto our territory, related to the gryphon who was the cause of the war, we will offer you shelter, but you will be watched, closely, by guards. We will decide what to do with you later. For now follow us back." I pushed down any doubt, I had felt before.

I turned to seek approval from Queen Aloha. She nodded and looked very proud, as we guided the prince back to the campsite, surrounding him, so he wouldn't be able to escape, or be seen. His smug look disgusted me, though, as he looked so stupid.

We soon landed, back in the jungle, and called our guards over, who guided the prince to a leafy bed, and sat down in a chair beside him, as he laid down and stretched out. Sighing dramatically, he complained, "It's not hot enough here!" He was flopping his head around as if he was in misery. Gryphons began to gather around us asking what happened. Queen Aloha began to explain it all, giving me a chance to rest.

I noticed Darklight and Ryuu in the crowd, listening quietly, as Queen Aloha quickly explained the situation. After she was done, yells of argument came from the crowd, one of them from Bonzer. Bonzer was a cranky, old gryphon, who always slept in late, always spoke his mind, and hated social life. "How can our queen be so naive, to shelter the idiot that started this war!" Bonzer bellowed. Roars of agreement came from the crowd, as they began yelling and fighting.

"ENOUGH!" Queen Aloha yowled The whole village went silent; the queen had never yelled at her subjects, like that, before.

They stood, shocked, and looked at each other, as they quieted down to listen to what the queen had to say. "We will decide what to do with the prince later, but for now treat him as one of your own. That's final... those who disagree, can bite their own tongue off." she growled, angrily, turning to leave before any other gryphon could get in a last word. The gryphons began to go back to work, some of them mummering, and others muttering, about this situation, unhappily.

I sighed and rushed off to find Honeysuckle, Grapefruit, and Queen Aloha. They had started talking about what to do with the gryphon prince. I settled down to listen. "We keep him here for the night, then we bring the Desert Gryphon royal family here, in the morning, so they can see him, for themselves." Honeysuckle suggested, looking in the direction of the prince's territory, while adjusting her glasses.

We all looked at each other with the same thought. This is the only way. The day passed quickly, as we gathered, armor and grabbed spears, just in case the Desert Gryphons wanted to battle when we reached the outskirts of their neighboring kingdom. We headed out, first thing in the morning. Desert guards greeted us at the border. "We got your letter,' they said; the Queen is here," and they stepped aside, to reveal the Desert Queen, standing there. She had a death glare in her eyes.

"My son is dead. Accept it," she said, turning to leave. Queen Aloha ran up and grabbed her by her shoulder. "Please, Amber, just come to the jungle. You need to see for yourself, in order to believe it." Queen Aloha looked so sincere, the Desert Queen saw no choice but to accept. We got ready and went on our way.

The Queen Amber flew beside Queen Aloha, looking quite upset and bothered. She kept glancing back at her guards, but they didn't seem to notice. What was going on? I wondered.

I bit my tongue, not wanting to further upset the Desert Gryphon Queen. We soon arrived at the jungle. The heir stood up from his small leaf bed, yawning.

Then, he and the queen locked eyes. The heir froze, dropping his food from his talons. He stood motionless, as if he was inside an iceberg. "M-M-Mother?" the heir asked, stuttering, and taking a step back. The Queen Amber dropped all of her royal things and raced to him, grabbing her son in a tight hug.

The heir seemed shocked, but sunk down into his mother's wings. She then moved him away. "Thorn, I thought you died? Please explain this all to me," she plead, holding her son in her talons, trembling. He sighed, and then began to explain.

"Ok, so what happened was, when traveling with my royal guard, I got ambushed by the Night Gryphon queen, and her guards. To survive, I and the guard swapped armor and jewels, because we sort of looked alike, they thought they had killed me. But I knew I couldn't return home, then, so I hid until all of them had gone, and I flew away that night, so no other gryphon would notice me." He finished, with a sigh, while looking down.

He felt guilty for the death of his guard. "He died a good death, defending his royalty," his mother said, comforting him. Prince Thorn sighed and fell into his mother's wings, once again.

"I want this war to end. But in order for it to end, we need to stop those Night Gryphons ... all they want is to dominate rule over our home," Prince Thorn said, standing back up, on his feet. His mother nodded. "I agree with my son, but how?" she asked, looking up at the sky. "I have an idea." Queen Aloha said with a smile.

We followed her, to the biggest rock we could see, and got on top. It looked over our whole campsite. Gryphons, there, talked and ate fruit, while others cared for gryphons, who were injured by the fire attack. For once, I began to notice all the pain our tribe had endured, as Gryphons surrounded each other, caring for each other's wounds, and sharing stories.

Queen Aloha was just about to call the tribe over, to discuss the situation, when a horrid scream of grief came from the 'healers' hut. We rushed over, worried we had been attacked again. As we entered, we saw the healers and medics, holding back a female gryphon. Her eyes were red with tears, and her feathers had turned to a dull white of grief and pain.

She had her talons reaching out, while the healers kept ahold of her. The medics had managed to get her to sit down, outside. The medics noticed us and nodded. We walked in, and saw a gryphon laying, limp, upon a leafy bed. His eyes were blank, staring forwards. His body laid there, in the leafy bed, with burn marks and claw marks covering his neck and back.

I noticed a necklace around his neck. It was a little silver circle with golden trim. I asked about it, and the medics handed me the necklace. As I opened it, I saw a picture of him and the grieving gryphon, together... only the female was a gryphonnet, beaming with joy and laughter, as the gryphon who owned this, now, lifeless body, was holding her and smiling.

My heart sank, as I realized, the gryphon lying dead was the father of the female gryphon sitting outside.

Her name was sunflower, I learned, from the name written on the back of the necklace. I clipped it back together, swallowing my surprise.

Queen Aloha seemed to already understand and led the way, as we made our way to Sunflower. Queen Aloha just shook her head, and handed Sunflower the necklace. Sunflower got herself together and walked away, with the necklace, her head hung low. She seemed to drag herself with every bit of her energy. A feeling of empathy creeped upon me as I watched Sunflower leave. "We must announce the death of our oldest elder, Aster," the Desert Queen said, and Prince Thorn nodded, both, understanding how it felt to lose one of your subjects.

We made our way to the rock as Queen Aloha called upon Our tribe. They all began to gather, shock waves rippling through the tribe, as they heard of the death of Aster. Queen Aloha began to speak.

"Tonight, we are here to grieve our lost elder, Aster. He was a loyal and loving father, brother, warrior and teacher. We will bury him tomorrow, for those who want to spend one last night with him. You may say your goodbyes tonight. We will bury *all* of our loved ones, who were lost in the fire, and we'll need to start early. We can decide what to do about Prince Thorn, tomorrow, as well.." Queen Aloha invited Queen Amber to spend the night. "Until it's decided, treat him, and his mother, like you would treat a friend," Queen Aloha finished, turning to leave, before any voice could argue.

Most of the elders stayed with Aster, cleaning his wounds and singing to him. My heart hung in my chest, watching them, but I was never close to him, so I knew I couldn't share his final night with them. Many gryphons had died in that fire, but we only had *time* to grieve Aster. A heavy feeling of exhaustion ran through my body, as I laid down to sleep. I made myself comfortable, and drifted off to a well-needed slumber.

Chapter t Ten

Unwelcomed Crimson Rose

Morning came quickly. After grabbing a bite to eat, I helped the others carry all the bodies of our tribe members, who died from the fire, to an appropriate spot, for burial. Sweat dripped down my head and back, as we carried the dead, walking quite a distance. We found a sweet little plain area, with plenty of flowers. "We'll bury Aster, and a few others, here... you guys find another spot for the rest," I said. They nodded and spoke no words, as they turned their backs, with the dead bodies hanging from them.

I began to dig, as sweat now poured from my forehead. It took some time. Hours passed, before we had everyone buried, along with stones, and their names plastered on them. I looked down at Aster's grave, before leaving. I grabbed a pile of rosemary and tulips, planting them atop his grave, "You can watch them grow," I whispered, resting my forehead on the face of the stone. "I will protect your daughter, Aster. Now, this is goodbye; rest in peace."

We flew back to our camp; it was almost sundown. We had, yet another night in this camp, we made, before we returned home. As I approached the awaiting camp, I noticed Queen Aloha, standing beside Prince Thorn, and his mother, the Desert Queen, Amber, patiently awaiting my arrival.

I softly landed on the hard rock ground. Looking up at them, I could see the pain, concern, worry, and overwhelming doubt. "It's not your fault." I blurted out, before I knew what I was doing. Thorn looked caught off guard but quickly got himself together. "I'm fine," he sighed, "Let's just get this over with." Prince Thorn muttered, and looked away from me.

I sighed in annoyance. Queen Aloha stepped up to the edge of the rock, calling upon her tribe. Soon, everyone was gathered below the rock. They all looked as if they hadn't gotten any sleep, as, while we were all working to bury the dead, others worked all day to take care of gryphonnets, that were so used to the fruit filled forest, being worry free. "My gryphons," Queen Aloha began, "we must end this horrible war, at any cost." All of the gryphons looked up, as if knowing their queen will guide them to victory, and save their families.

"I've been traveling, and I know this," she continued. "The Sky Wing Gryphons have joined with the Night Gryphons, in this war, but the *Sea* Gryphons have, now, joined us!" Just as she said that, the Sea Gryphon army, along with the Gryphon Fins army, landed down, on both sides. The queen of the Sea Gryphons stepped forward. "My army is in your hands, Queen Aloha," the Sea Queen said, dipping her head, in respect. "Hello, Queen Oasis," Aloha said, walking up to the Sea Gryphon queen, and offering her hand.

"Hello Queen Angler," she also said, turning to the Gryphon Fins queen. All three of the queens stood together, looking down upon Sea Gryphons, Gryphon Fins, and Jungle Gryphons, alike.

Queen Aloha stepped up, with Queen Oasis and Queen Angler, behind her, on either side. "Gryphons, all! We will win this war, even if it means to rid our homeland of the Night Gryphons, once and for all! Come together! Together we have fire power, camouflage, and sea disguise! Together, we are unstoppable!

"We are doing this for our loved ones... for our children's lives and future, and for our home!" Queen Aloha yelled, with passion, raising her talons into the air, in a fist. "Now, go get some rest and start battle planning. We fight, come tomorrow." Queen Aloha said, turning her back to the tribes.

Before leaving, she turned her head, to look at her subjects, once more. "Make your families proud," she said, and with that, she left, to chat with the elders. I walked down to find Ryuu and Darklight. As I came closer, a light, behind the shadow of a gryphon, blinded me. I rubbed my eyes and blinked away the light spots. I saw Ryuu's eyes, puffy with red tears hugging the gryphon. Wait, is it a ghost? I began to notice the details in the gryphon's scales. I recognized the ruby-red eyes, the golden brown scales, sharp spikes, the body shape and the smile. "Ruby! Your back!" I yelled tears streaming down my face.

I threw myself into the hug with Ryuu and Ruby. "I'm so glad you came back, I missed you so, *so* much!" I said, smiling bigger than I ever had, "How could I go on without my two boys?" Ruby asked, grinning and wrapping her wings around both of us.

She said, she had been watching us the whole time, but a gryphon, who seemed to have animus powers, saw her and granted her wish to have others see her, so she had been going around seeing her family and friends again. Her eyes started to tear up. "I missed you guys so much... seeing you two in pain, after I died is the worst thing that ever happened to me," she said, choking on air, and sobbing, while hugging us tighter.

Soon, after I had filled Ruby in, on all that had been happening, she appeared shocked. "Wait! But we

won the battle! We killed the Night Gryphon queen!"
Ruby yelled. Then, I remembered something Queen
Aloha had told me. "Yes, but her *daughter* inherited the
throne," I stated. "She had the Ice Gryphons join her
tribe, and declared war on both our tribe and the Desert
Gryphons, so we came together, and the Sea Gryphons
joined us," I explained, to answer Ruby's question.

Ruby stopped and sighed, "I promise you, we'll
win this war, and we'll do it for our families." Ruby said
goodbye and flew off to find others, she'd missed. I and
Ryuu headed over to talk to the queens. Queen Oasis,
Queen Angler and Queen Aloha, all sat together, battle
planning. "I have a plan," I said, as we approached them.
They stopped their conversation, giving me a warm
welcome. Ryuu and I bowed our heads, in response,
before starting. I looked around and sighed, "Okay,
here's my plan... we attack *tonight*.

"We have a group of Gryphon Fins go in
disguised, as the gryphon royal guard so they'll be let
into their battle planning... they will take their maps and

come back here to us, at the border, as our armies will be camping in the bordering mountains.

"We will figure out their battle plans and when they are most weak, then we will go in, we will drug all the guards and bring all of them to the border to rest... the guards should stay asleep for a minimum of ten hours, and when they wake up, it will take them a while to regain their strength because the drug will drain their energy. That will leave the Night Gryphons defenseless and then, we'll send another group to drug the Ice Gryphon guards, as well." I finished, sighing in a big breath of air.

The queens looked at each other, thoughtfully, and after debating, Queen Aloha stepped up to me. "Okay, she said... let's do it." The night came, as we made our way to the palace. My group sat down at the border, by the Night Gryphons' kingdom, with another group, while the others headed out to the *Ice K*ingdom, to start carrying out the plan.

Hours of waiting and tension held at our throats, as we waited for our gryphon spy group to return. "Come on in guys, huddle," one gryphon called, and we all came together. "Alright guys... as soon as the guys out there return, we are heading out. Here, use these to drug the guards, in their rooms, as they sleep. Be sure not to make a sound." As he finished, the Gryphon Fins arrived.

The gryphon, in front, came forward, "Jungle, what do you have?" he asked. Jungle sighed happily, "Ok, so Bonzer, we found out they are planning to attack us in the morning... they have armor ready waiting outside the guards quarters, and they are gonna attack us from three different angles, so if we destroy their armor while we're there, they will be easily taken down in the morning," Jungle reported. Bonzer nodded in agreement. "Alright guys, when we get there, drug the guards and take the armor."

We nodded and took off into the sky, the air flowed by us, as we flew side by side, quieter than a mouse. The palace sat before us. We landed, and made our way inside. The halls were empty and tall. A sudden huge slam came from down the hall. We looked back and forth, stunned, "You guys stay here, I'll go check it out," I whispered. The others ran to hide, as I raced forwards. Tension grew, as I got closer and closer.

I began to hear laughing and banging, "Hey!" I yelled, turning to face a gryphon, a gryphon that had been laughing on their back while holding a mirror, smiling at themself. A sudden smell of blood filled the air. I turned to see a random, old gryphon, lying dead on the ground, with its neck slit open.

"Oh my god! Watch where you step, there is a dead body next to you!" I yelled, stepping in the way. The odd gryphon laughed, "Oh him? I killed him. Saw him bothering my friend, so, I just cut his neck open... I'm Abyss, by the way; who are you?" they asked, turning back to the mirror, they held in their talons.

But, before we could answer, they continued. "You know, I saw you guys, at the border, and didn't tell anyone... because I want to help you guys! I cannot wait to have so much fun killing Night Gryphons and drugging them!" they excitedly said, turning to face me, again. I hesitated, but, not wanting them to ruin our plan, I sighed and agreed, "Alright, I'm Noirscales. Now don't make a sound; wait for us outside the palace and *try* not to kill anyone while we're gone." Abyss nodded, and raced out.

I explained the situation to everyone else; they understood, and sent someone out to tell *those at the ice kingdom*. Hours passed... we got all the guards out. We threw them into a cave. "Hey gryphons ! Can you use this metal and build some jail bars?" Queen Aloha asked. They nodded and got to work. By the morning all the guards had been put in caves with jail bars to keep them in there and the armor they had made was given to the soldiers. I sighed and fell to the ground glad that we had finished. "Noirscales. Over here!" Bonzer called from far away, I turned toward him... a scout of gryphons was getting ready to leave, they were loading up with spears, knives, and armor. I walked over and Dust noticed me, "here.." she smiled, handing me a bag of armor, spears, and knives. I thanked her and slid into the armor, loading the knives into the knife pockets and the spears in their cases, on the armor.

We all exchanged looks, knowing some of us might *not* make it out of here alive, because the royal families of the Night Gryphons and Ice Gryphons, are the most brutal of us all. "We'll be okay," Dust said, taking my talons in hers. I sighed, terrified to let out all the fear, pent up in my mind... and thanked her. She smiled and we all shared the same thought, while taking off into the air... if we die, then we die a worthy death. I led the way, as we flew in the brightness of the day. The palace stood before us, tall and proud. That palace is better than the gryphons that live in it, I thought, to myself, bitterly. Choking on the thoughts in my mind, as it raced through billions of possibilities, while the warm wind brushed against my wings, guiding the others on, to our final destination.

The hard rock ground felt cold under our sharp

talons. "This is it," Dust whispered in my ear, as we sneaked in, through the window, to the dining room. "I know," I said, "I promise you we can do this. I'm not gonna let us die," trying to reassure Dust, and the rest of the group, even though, it was *not* enough to hide my *own* doubts. We quietly made our way into the Night royals' room. The family was fast asleep.

I asked, "What do we do now? Do we kill them in their sleep, or take them hostage?" Our commander spoke up... "We wake them; I want to have a real fight," he growled. He nodded and shot fire, onto their beds, to wake them up. The young queen jolted awake. "Who are you?!" she demanded to know. She called out to her father, the king, while throwing water on the fire; the king woke his son. They all stared at us, not with fear, but with rage and annoyance.

I stepped forward, "You should recognize me... sister," I said, taking a bitter tone. Her face froze, as I stepped into the light, so she could see my face. "I thought *my* mother *killed* you!" she scowled, lashing her tail and looking around, at her family, desperately, for help. "It doesn't matter," she snarled... "you're not my brother, anymore, traitor!" With that, she pounced and lashed her tail, smacking my side. The pain wretched, as she pinned me down by my throat. "You are **not** my brother," she said bitterly, digging her talons, further, into my neck. The pain sharpened, but I was not weak!

Images of Darklight laughing and playing, her first hunt, her first word... came flooding into my mind. I knew I had to survive, for her sake. I shoved my sister off me, flipping her over, onto her back. "I'm not letting you ruin my life! I have friends, I have family and I have a little sister! You're not ruining this for me!" I said. "Now!" I yelled. Dust shot the tranquilizer at the young queen. Her body went limp, almost immediately, as she fell into unconsciousness. We then tranquilized the king and the prince.

As we began to tie up the royal family, our commander stepped up, and said, "we need to throw these three in prison and get some answers, when they come to," flashing his wings aggressively, before leading us away, while we carried the limp royals.

I carried the prince. He had lots of scars and beat up scales. I kinda felt bad for him. He must've gone through a lot of pain to end up like this. No, don't feel bad... he has the part of the family, I would have had, if he didn't exist. He stole it from me, I thought to myself, bitterly. But, I soon realized, I would not have wanted to be a member of that family, anyway.

We arrived back, at the mountains. We landed, laying the tranquilized royals onto the ground, to be put into the separate cave prisons we'd created. From all of the, yelling and fighting, we could hear, I guessed the drugged guards had woken up, and were not pleased with the situation.

"What did you do to our Queen?!" one of the guards yelled. He was up against the bars, with his stretched out talons, ready to claw any gryphon who came near. I shuddered. He had horrible burns across his body. The skin seamed the curl and looked as if he had fallen into a volcano. His spikes along the back were a dark midnight color as they pointed straight up off his spine, as he lashed his tail, yelling insults. I watched in horror, as one of our guards ran over and shot him in one of his legs, with a poisonous dart.

His screams echoed down the halls, as he yelped in pain, falling to the ground, while the poison began eating away, at the skin on his leg, quickly destroying it. His eyes writhed with pain, as he was screaming and yelling. He, eventually, passed out from shock.

His screams stayed in my mind for a while. I looked over and noticed Queen Aloha, looking guilty. I came to her side, "You did what you had to do," I softly said, comforting her, as she looked down at the forest floor. Rain began to pour down on us. We waited in silence, as the rain was seen as a symbol that *we are almost at peace.*

I took a moment and went over the list, in my head, of all the lost lives. A sigh escaped my throat. I looked up and the rain ran down my face.

Then, I felt the rain stop and my face began to dry. I looked up, and saw a wing, shielding me from the rain. "It's quite cold out here," a sweet, deep voice, softly said. I looked up to see Ryuu standing beside me. His warm face beamed in the light of the moon. "You know, we're really lucky to still be alive right now, he said, "and you need to stay alive for Darklight. She needs you, and you know that, but you just brush it off, and think she'll be okay without you. She really won't, you are her world."

His words echoed in my mind, "I know." I sighed, and a brief smile crossed my face. "Come on... let's go get some rest; tomorrow we go home. "Oh, and Ryuu," I said, before turning to leave, "Thank you." Ryuu smiled and softly nodded his head. We walked away together wing in wing

I looked up at Ryuu's face, he was smiling, though his eyes showed clear signs of grief. I wanted to throw my arms around Ryuu and tell him everything would be okay, like he would do for me, but, I knew he needed to learn how to process his feelings on his own.

Chapter Eleven

Golden Heart

The next morning, we arrived back at our hut, in the Jungle village. Darklight jumped into my arms, as I, and Ryuu, walked in. "I saw Ruby!" she exclaimed happily, her eyes shining in the light of day. Ryuu gave a soft smile, and laid down at the other end of the hut. I picked up Darklight, and swirled her around in the air, and she began to laugh. "Big brother, stop!" she giggled. I chuckled and set her down.

"Wanna go with the group that is going out to collect food for the tribe?" I asked her, unexpectedly. She nodded, and hugged me, before running off. Then, I sighed. "Smart idea, sending her away. She would be sad to see how overworked and stressed, as you have been lately," Ryuu said, turning to face me.

I laid down beside him. It has been almost a month since I gave our queen the prophecy that ended up saving us from the fire attack. Ever since then, we hadn't gotten a chance to be at rest. I sighed, looking upwards as the starlight shone through open windows. Jars of honey suckle danced in the wind, as a breeze traveled through the campsite.

A feeling of sadness creeped up on me, knowing that all of this could, easily, be ruined by another attack. I promise, I won't let that happen, I said to myself, clutching my talons to my chest. Ryuu put his talons on my shoulder and looked at me, his forest-green eyes locked in contact with mine. For a moment, I had forgotten about all the pain and stress in my life. We stayed like that for a small while, letting our worries fade, as we looked deep into each other's colorful, and exploring eyes. A sigh of happiness escaped my throat, as I fell to sleep, in Ryuu's wings.

I was awakened, when another gryphon fell onto me. I looked up to see Dust. She looked horridly frantic, as panic and worry were clear in her face. We stood up in a hurry, and Dust led us outside, to other gryphons gathering around the middle of the campsite.

Not a word was being spoken. Then, we saw a limp gryphon body in the clearing. Queen Oasis hung her head low, and cried, by the body of her son, Prince Thorn. She began to scream up at the sky, "Why?! Why take my son from me now?! He was all I had left!" she wailed, and we stared at each other, knowing that the pain she was going through *was* traumatizing.

Queen Aloha and Queen Angler came to her side, putting their wings around her. No gryphon dared to speak... as a royal loved-one had been lost. After a few hours, the gryphons began to go back to their daily routine. I knew it was easier for them, since they didn't know the prince that well.

Even though I'd only met him a few weeks ago, I felt a small piece of my heart had broken when he died. Queen Oasis approached me and Ryuu. Her face was red, eyes, puffy from crying. She hung low, in the air, as she neared. Unexpectedly, she hugged me. A wave of shock hit me, like a wall.

A royal Queen, who always made sure others respected her, broke down and hugged me, as she sobbed. After what seemed like a good while, she removed herself from the embrace, and spoke to me, in a shaking voice, "Thorn wanted me to give this to you, please take care of it."

She opened her talons, and grabbed mine in hers, placing a necklace in my palm. It was a long black rope, wrapped with golden thread, with a tiny emerald, hanging from it, in a golden cast. This golden object, in the shape of a heart, while it looked so simple, held huge significance. I thanked the queen, and we hurried off.

Back at Ryuu's hut, sitting side by side, talking, we contemplated the day... "So Thorn is really dead, now - what do we do?" Ryuu questioned, sighing. He picked up his wooden cup and looked around, expectantly. Darklight jumped up onto the chair beside us, and she beamed with thoughtful eyes. "I know!" Darklight said, waving her talons in the air. So, Ryuu nodded, giving her a chance to speak.

She smiled, thankfully, before starting... "Okay, so, now the prince is really dead, but we don't know who killed him; let's send troops out to search the grounds, and his body, for any hint of who killed him. After we figure that out, we either banish them, if they are on our own... or, if they are not, then we launch an attack!"

Darklight jumped up, swiping at the air, as if attacking an enemy gryphon. Then, Ryuu looked at me, and said, "You've got quite a smart sister." Smiling now, his bright eyes were beaming. "Also... yeah, let's do that." Ryuu said, turning to Darklight, and patting her on her head, to praise her.

We spent the night together, talking away hours, our voices fading into the darkness of the night, as it creeped upon us. "I'm going to get some sleep, and you guys should too," Ryuu yawned, waving his talons at his yawning mouth. He then took Darklight by the talons and led her to her bed. Ryuu came back, stood in front of his bed, looking down, and a dreadful frown crossed his face, as he looked back at me, his eyes, once again, locking into mine. "I am counting on you to keep Darklight safe. There is something behind that necklace. I know it." His voice stood frozen in the air, as his seriousness scared me. He always smiled, chuckled and laughed when he talked, but now, I could tell he really meant it. "What are you saying?!" I demanded, with worry in my voice. He flopped onto the bed, giving me one last glance, before drifting off to sleep.

Why won't he answer me! I thought to myself, in frustration. No, don't worry about that... he's your friend; he's trying to keep you alive and okay. "Oh why must you be so complicated?" I said, soothingly, while putting leafy quilt over Ryuu's sleeping body.

He slept so peacefully, as he breathed in a comforting pattern. I stood there, looking up at the window... a thought came to me. I need to get out of here, and I quickly grabbed a piece of scroll. My talons shook, as I dipped the feather into ink. I then started writing, and, as each word was written, memories flashed in my head. "Dear Ryuu and my dear sister, Darklight:"

I started closing my eyes. I remembered back, at me and Darklight, as children, running through fields of flowers, laughing and giggling, without a care in the world. Chasing each other down at the berry-picking mountains, shoving our faces with strawberries, and joking, while tackling each other, as if we were strong, loyal members of the army. No scars and no worries, just gryphonnets, having fun.

I would do anything to have that feeling back, again. I dipped the feather into the dark ink, once more, and began my writing again... "I love both of you very much, but I have targets on my back; the Night Gryphons are coming for me. The longer I stay with you two, the more danger I put you in. If you're attacked by the gryphons, who are coming after me, there is a trap door in Darklight's room, leading to an underground bunker. Go in there, and wait, until they are gone. "I love you both, sincerely... Noirscales."

A deep sigh exhaled, as I looked up at the night sky. I have to do this, I thought to myself. "Farewell, my friends," I said.to all, my voice, alone in the night. The future awaits, I thought, as I stepped out. The wind brushed by the trees, which stood in the night, tall and watching. Not a single noise sounded in the village.

I told myself, I have to end this war, for my family and friends, especially Ryuu and Darklight. The night seemed to swallow me whole, as I left my home. Go, be free, and leave this war behind, a voice in my head said. I began to picture making new friends, enjoying time flying together, picking berries, playing in the field.

Stop! You need to do this, I told myself. A sudden crack sounded beside me, "Oh wonderful... you finally show your face," a voice said. I turned to the gryphon now behind me. They flew in the shadows, a crazy smile, crossing their face, had long scars, in their wings, with blood, stained in their scales. Something scared me, as I made contact with bloodshot-red eyes.

They began to laugh uncontrollably, swinging a knife around in the air, blood dripped from it, and they continued to laugh. I landed; and they followed.

"What do you want? Why do you keep following me?!" I yelled, standing my ground, gripping the grass under my talons, ripping it free of the dirt.

"Oh I'm just having some fun! I don't wanna hurt a *prince*," they giggled, holding talons to their mouth... "or, maybe I would." Then they stepped out of the shadows, and I fell back, in shock.

"Abyss! What?! It was you!" I exclaimed, as he stood in front of me, smiling while holding the knife. Abyss began to, slowly, cut a line in their palm, just watching, as the blood fell. While it dripped onto the ground, Abyss breathed in the blood-filled air.

Chapter Twelve

<u>Shadowed Maniac</u>

"Blood is such a funny thing!" he said, "sometimes a little comes out, and other times, oops... there goes your life!" Abyss sighed, turning to face me, "Sometimes, it's just better to never speak again." Abyss smirked, with a smug face, raising their knife into the air.

"Get away from me!" I yelled, shoving him down under my talons. He looked up at me, scoffing, "I'm not gonna hurt you, just let me tag along," he said. As he escaped my grip, and wiped the dirt off their dark, violet wings, I stepped back. He sound so sincere, I thought, hesitating, with questionable worry holding me, by my throat. "Fine, I'll trust you," I said, muttering under my breath, while Abyss smiled, now satisfied,

Wonderful!" he said, waving his wings out dramatically. Ugh, why is he so *over the top*? I wondered. "Well, let's get moving then," I said, turning to look up at the brimming night sky, as the sun was starting to climb its way up the horizon.

"We don't have much time, and I don't want anyone to see us leaving. As soon as we make our way out, we will find Prince Thorn's killer." Abyss looked over at me, confused for a second, before an obvious expression of realization hit his face. "Oh! The dead gryphon?" Abyss asked, excited he knew who I was talking about.

I glared at them... how they could be so happy, and energetic, right now, when our ally just lost an heir? Abyss didn't seem to get it, and started watching a butterfly, as it flew up and around a small plant, growing, hanging from the edge of a beautiful oak tree. But, by the time the sun was up in the sky, Abyss and I had made it out of the village, without being seen.

We stopped to rest outside of a cave... just a small nap, I thought to myself. A sigh escaped my lungs, as I looked back up in the sky. Clouds, slowly, moved over me, floating in the sky, helplessly, like little puffs of cotton. The sun shone down, through the clouds, lighting up our gloomy world.

A sudden shock went through my body. It felt as if something had zapped me. I looked down to see a ray of sunlight, hitting the emerald, of the necklace Thorn had given me. A raspy voice began to speak.

It said, "A forbidden sky, and rain, has taken the life of a sand gryphon... finding the answer, harbored in the home of ice and night." Was the necklace talking to me!? I panicked. I immediately knew Abyss could *not* know about this, but what did it mean? Did a *special* gryphon hybrid kill the prince? Well, if that's what it is, that's where our hunt begins.

"You okay? You stood up really quickly and you looked totally freaked out!" Abyss asked, as they walked toward me with a concerned look crossing their face.

I shrugged in response, "It's nothing really, the stone just got really hot." I brushed my leg off, to make it seem more real. Abyss leaned down near the stone, "Yeesh! You're right it's getting too hot out here.

Come inside the cave. I brought us some food."

I smiled, as we walked inside together, "So, how are we gonna find the killer? Can I stab 'em, when we find 'em?" Abyss questioned, excitedly, chomping down fiercely on their share of the cow. I grunted in irritation. "We are *not* killers," I said, trying to get the point across, that I would not let Abyss kill whenever they wanted, around me, "I'm the one in charge here, and I say no killing, Okay?"

Abyss muttered something under his breath, with a disappointed countenance." "Fine," he said. I smiled, satisfied that my lie had worked, "Now here's our plan."

I began to explain my plan, for how we were going to sneak into the middle of the Ice Kingdom, in search of a special hybrid gryphon "How do you know what type of gryphon?" Abyss asked, with a look, that I could tell was pure suspicion. "Oh, the royal guard and I talked about it, before we left," I said, confidently, praying they'd fall for my second stupid lie. Abyss nodded, eyeing me slightly, "Well I'm gonna get some sleep, now,

I'm exhausted!" he said, stretching out and falling onto one of the leaf beds, we had set up, as if there was no tomorrow and they gave up on life. I laughed at their dramatic act. "You're a handful, aren't you?" I remarked. "Alright get some sleep; I'll be guarding."

I sat outside the cave, very bored. There was nothing to watch, really, but I knew I couldn't sleep. Birds flew over me, dancing on the current of the wind, chirping loudly, swinging around each other, feathers brushing against feathers.

Memories of Ryuu flashed in front of me, his smile... the way he talked on and on, for hours, the way he would laugh and play, so happily, with Darklight. I began to realize, even more, how much I cared, the farther away I traveled. A stinging pain dropped on my heart, as I knew I could not return, yet, in order to keep my loved ones safe. "Finally, you're all alone.." a deep voice said, from amongst the shadows. I sighed, "Who are you, and what do you want?" Yawning, I turned, to face a *mysterious* gryphon.

Only their eyes, were visible, as they wore a shaggy cloak with a hood, partially covering their face. Their stone black eyes pierced me, like a thousand swords. "I'm Falcon," this figure said... "I've come to finish my mission."

I looked around in confusion, before realization hit me like a rock. "Are you the assassin, I'm looking for?!" I gasped... "the one who killed Prince Thorn!?" Stepping back, I felt that I had reached the end of the cliff, behind me. I knew my wing was broken, so I would not be able to fly away very fast... come on, Noirscales, think! I shouted, at myself.

"Abyss!" I yelled, towards the cave. "The assassin is here!" I screeched. "Oops... big mistake, Noirscales," Falcon said, reaching into the pocket of his cloak, pulling out a dagger. I noticed it had the design of rivers, embedded in the blade; I also noticed that this guy had many *weird* things, and lots of pockets to put them in, and the hood that scavengers wear... not gryphons. He walked forwards, shoving me down onto the hard rock, beneath us. I groaned in pain, as the rock stabbed into my neck... jagged edges, piercing through my scales.

"Who sent you!" I demanded to know, flinching from the pain in my neck. Just then, I felt a single tear make its way down my dry face, and disappear into the rock below. The weight of this attacker disappeared, suddenly, as Abyss yanked him off me.

I watched, as Abyss put a piece of wet paper over his mouth, while holding him back by his throat. Falcon struggled, for just a bit, and reached out, yelling from under the paper, before his eyes rolled back, and he fell fast asleep. His limp body hit the stone with a thud, as Abyss let him go, and walked over and helped me up, while Falcon lay there, harmless.

Are you okay, Noirscales?" Abyss asked... "Uh, not like I would care, though," he quickly added, before I could even answer. I could tell they were hiding a soft spot. I let out a small chuckle, and picked Falcon up, hoisting him onto my back. But then I heard a voice behind me... "Let Falcon go!" and an *odd-looking* gryphon leapt at me, with bloodthirsty eyes. As it yelled, it knocked Flacon out of my grip and tackled Abyss.

"Hey!" I said, glaring, "who are you anyways?!" The smell of fresh blood filled the air, as the wind was blowing across the horizon. The battle raged, gryphon against gryphon, talons in the air, lashing and clawing, scarring one another. As the odd gryphon raised their talons in the air, my vision blurred.

Everything began to go dark. I began to weaken, as the odd gryphon bent down and whispered in my ear, "My name is Aardvark, of the Night Gryphons ." Just then, I felt a sharp pain in my left side, and everything went black.

I began to blink my eyes open, adjusting to the morning light. As my body began to wake, I heard gryphons, crying and talking. I turned to see Abyss, talking to Ryuu and Darklight, who's eyes were puffy and red, with tears. I knew I was back at home, but was too weak to protest. "Abyss… what happened?" I asked, weakly, raising my head, to see the three clearer.

Ryuu looked shocked, and was knocking things down as he raced to my side, collapsing upon me, he threw his wings around me, "Oh, Noirscales... we thought we lost you forever! Don't ever do that again!"

His words were so simple, yet they were spoken with such a painful voice. I hugged him, and smiled, glad to be back in his scarlet-red-feathered wings. He looked so sad, it broke my heart. "Look at yourself..." Ryuu said, quietly, his eyes, tearing up again.

I reached up and wiped Ryuu's tears, before turning to look down, at my body. I froze, when I saw my torso, covered in nasty scars. One cut was all the way across my left side. It had tons of leaf padding on it, to stop the bleeding, but, looked as if it had healed, somewhat, which must've taken some time.

"How long was I asleep?" I asked, still frozen, while staring at my scar. "You were out for almost a month, Noirscales, and if you didn't wake up soon you would've died," Darklight said, wiping tears, a soft smile crossing her face, while her gentle eyes told me all I needed to know. "Aardvark, the gryphon assassin, dropped you off, at my front door..." Ryuu explained. "You were covered in your own blood and already in a coma. All he said, before he left, was, "I was not assigned to kill Noirscales, so here - he can live, but don't let him get in my way again," adding, "I'm not a monster, I'm just smart."

I looked down, my talons scraping up the dirt below me, "I shouldn't have let him get away!" I said, with a new anger waking inside me. "Noirscales..." Ryuu said, reaching his talons out to me. I smacked them away, "I'm fine!" I yelled, getting up and running out of the hut, into the rain. Don't stop running, I thought. Tears rushed down my scarred face, as I ran, and Ryuu chased after me, desperately calling out my name.

I eventually collapsed to the ground, hiding my face in my talons, tensing my body in fear and shame. "I can do better than this!" I yelled, up at the sky, as I yanked grass out of the ground. I looked down at my talons, the grass in my palms, torn apart. I clenched my fist, letting tears stream down my face, as the sky began to cry, along with me.

The entire forest seemed to understand. "I'm sorry," I softly said, rolling over and touching my forehead to the ground, closing my eyes. I felt the rain stop and I looked up, to see scarlet-red wings shielding me from the drops, "It's okay to cry, just don't run away, Noirscales... many gryphons look up to you, and it's okay to feel pressured - you just have to learn how to face it." Ryuu's voice was calming, easing my worries.

I fell into his warm embrace, once again. "It's just all too much, sometimes," I said. "I'm glad I have you, and I know Ruby would be glad to see how much we've both grown." Leaning into Ryuu's shoulder, forgetting about the dreadful world around me, for the moment, I sighed out a cold breath, blowing it into the air, and watching it fade away. Then, I turned to face Ryuu... "Ryuu, I'm gonna end this war, once and for all," I stated, matter-of-factly, "and I beg you, no matter what happens to me, promise you will take good care of my little sister, Darklight, okay?" I was holding his talons in mine, as we locked eyes; his big, forest-green eyes melted my heart. Then he spoke, ever so softly, "I promise" Those simple words gave me the drive I needed to rid our lives of this terrible evil, forever.

Chapter Thirteen

A Past Discovered

The day of the final battle arrived, and thousands of gryphons lined the ground, wing to wing, armor, lined and labeled, with the tribal name, to which, they belong. Ice Gryphons and Night Gryphons, covered the mountainside, facing us, their piercing eyes glaring down, at the battle field below.

The Gryphon Fins lined the front of our field, with Desert gryphons and Sea gryphons, on either side of us. I stood up front, with Ryuu, Queen Aloha, Queen Oasis and Queen Angler, side by side, as they were waiting for the right time to give the command. A hush came across the armies, as the queens all got ready to speak.

"Go! Soldiers... attack!" they all shouted. As the words were spoken, the quiet hush turned into a raging battle, with gryphons screaming, some losing their lives.

I looked at Ryuu. "We can do this," I mouthed, smiling softly at him. A Night Gryphon raced toward him, before he could turn around. "Ryuu look out!" I screamed, feeling the ground open up and swallow me.

I watched, in horror, as Ryuu quickly swirled around... but the Night Gryphon was already on top of him. Ryuu's eyes widened as the enemy began to hold him down, by his neck, his sharp talons piercing Ryuu's skin. I felt my body freeze, while watching the only gryphon, who had loved me, for me, screaming in pain, laying, defenseless, under the Night Gryphon's talons.

"You're not taking my best friend!" I yelled, racing toward them, tackling the Night Gryphon. He fell to the ground, but quickly got up, slashing at my side. I grabbed him by the shoulder, forcefully, throwing him down onto the cold, hard ground, again and he let out an ear-piercing scream.

Then, I held his mouth open, taking in a deep breath, and shot fire straight down his throat. He tried to scream, again, but couldn't, and he punched at his neck, as the skin started to burn from the inside, out. Soon enough, he lay on the ground, dead. I quickly turned, collapsing to the ground beside Ryuu... he was laying there, weak, with holes in his neck, bleeding out... "no, no, no... stay with me. Come on, stay with me," I stuttered, choking on my own, sobbing gulps.

Ryuu took my talons in his. I locked eyes with him, once more. I felt my eyes sting, as they were filling with uncontrollable tears. "No... no! You are not gonna die, Ryuu! You're *not* gonna die. You promised, you'd stay!" I said, shaking, while holding his fragile body in my clumsy talons. I leaned him up against me, comforting him. I pulled out a few strands of grass, some cobwebs and small pieces of extra rope. "I'm not gonna let you die." I said, as I made bandages for his neck.

I looked down at him... his head laying in my lap and he smiled up at me, his cheeks more red than usual, as his feathers, faded to a light pink. "Noirscales," he said softly, "I'm *going* to die... accept it, but I have to tell you..." Ryuu took a breath, as I cut him off, "No! Don't talk like that, okay? I said, tears streaming down my traumatized face, "You're not gonna die!" "Noirscales," he said, sternly, "will you shut up and let me love you? you idiot! Isn't it obvious, I'm in love with you?!" I froze. The words he said, played on repeat in my mind, as I called doctors for Ryuu, and we left the battlefield.

He smiled at me, as the doctors looked him over and took him to be helped. I took a deep breath, going through an entire bundle of emotions. Did I *love him* too? I shook off the thought, as foolishness, though they stuck in the back of my mind, still repeating.

He's always been there for me, I recalled, staring down at my talons, and finding a new sense of happiness and pride. Hours of anxiety passed, as I waited for news.

Then, I saw a doctor come out of the room, "Doc, Is he okay?!" I asked, rushing up to him, my eyes showing my terror. He laughed, putting his talons on my shoulder, "He's fine, but, if you had waited any longer he would not have made it... you are a true hero," he said to me, "now go back out there and win this war."

I nodded, hugged the doctor, and rushed out, yanking out my knife. I noticed Abyss, laughing, as ten gryphons raced at him. He jumped up, plunging his knife down, and swinging his tail, his spikes stabbing *all ten* of the pursuing Night Gryphons. He looked very happy, and alive, blood covering his side, and wings, as he ran through the groups of Night and Ice Gryphons, taking lives easily.

I stared, in amazement, at Abyss' killing skills, as blood flew into the air around them, near any gryphon whose life was so easily taken, under the sharp claws of this maniac. I was not sure if I should be proud or worried.

Two Night Gryphons creeped up behind him, but I knew Abyss had already noticed they were there, before these gryphons jumped up to tackle him. Abyss swerved to the side; revealing that there was a bomb where they were fighting. "Good luck!" Abyss shouted, flying away, as the bomb blew up all of the gryphons around it. This part of the battle lasted only half an hour.

We had taken the win as the Night Ggryphons were abolished, one by one. As I looked upon the field, the only color I saw, was blood-red... and, of the scattered bodies that covered the ground, most were Night Gryphons and Ice Gryphons.

A few, were Gryphon Fins, and Desert Gryphons, and my eyes fell upon a group of Sea Gryphons, mourning over one of their own. I creeped over to see who it was, that laid on the ground there. As I got closer, shock took control, as there, on the cold ground, lay the dead body of Queen Oasis!

I noticed a young gryphon, curled up against her, sobbing... she looked a little ike the Queen - same eyes and frill – then, I remembered the Queen had a niece, and since her sister had already passed away, Queen Oasis was raising her.

Now that Queen Oasis, was gone... the throne would be left to her. The poor, little Sea Gryphon; she's barely twenty. Just a gryphonnet, really. I watched, as her tribe comforted her, while, also, sharing her grief.

I knew I couldn't join them, since she was not *my* Queen, though she was a loyal Queen... and though, I could not grieve *with* them, I paid my respects to her, on my own. Hours went by, while I joined the troops, in collecting the bodies, to be identified, all the while, hoping that I wouldn't come along the body of someone else I knew.

As dusk approached, all of the bodies, from our side, were identified, and buried in the nearby graveyard. Then, I noticed Ryuu among the crowds, so I rushed to his side, quickly. He had long bandages wrapped on his neck, with padding underneath, but he was okay. "Oh thank the tribes you're okay!" I said, throwing my wings around Ryuu, pulling him into a bear hug, after which, we both chuckled and began heading back home. Back to a home of peace and love, I thought to myself, smiling.

I noticed Queen Aloha walking over to us, as we headed out... she looked very pleased with herself, as her feathers shone a bright yellow, glowing with pride. She greeted us with a slight nod. She opened her leather pouch, and pulled out a fragile paper. I was surprised to see it... it was the prophecy I had delivered to her, moons ago. The queen began to talk very carefully, making sure we were paying close attention. "This prophecy," she said, "told me what I had to do, in order to keep our tribes alive, and how to end this war... but it, also, told me how more lives would have been destroyed, and how Jungle Gryphons would have been in agony, if the war was not handled properly. So, I want to thank you, Noirscales, you saved *everyone* here."

As she praised me, a smile crossed my face. I thanked her, surprised to be praised by the queen. Then, she sighed and confessed something that changed my entire world. "Noirscales," she said... "I have to tell you something. Queen Bluemoon was *not really* your mother." She went on, "There was a sweet, little gryphon, named Ambi, who was exiled from the *Night Kingdom*, having been framed, for murder, so she took refuge, here, for a while.

She was pregnant, and died, shortly after she had you, and I promised her, I would look after you, for her. She was a wise gryphon... a healer. She knew all kinds of herb mixtures, and became our best medic in many years, delivered prophecy whenever she could, saved countless lives and told countless stories.

Shortly before your birth, our kingdom fell into crisis, and she promised, she would bring a miracle to save our home. "I never realized it, until now, Noirscales... but, that miracle, was you," Queen Aloha said, smiling.

I was relieved to know that I wasn't related to that horrible monster, Queen Bluemoon, but I wished I could have met my real mother... if only I could see the dead. Just then, Queen Aloha told me something else, that made it all make sense. "Ever wonder why your coloring is paler and more white than other gryphons?" she asked. "It's because your father was a *purebred* gryphon, so you are a *special* hybrid." Her words sent a shocking chill through my veins. So, am I not who I think I am?

To Be Continued...